D1175922

SAINT LOUIE BLUES

Also by Jake Tanner

Old Black Magic

JAKE TANNER
—A B.F. HOPPER MYSTERY—

SAINT LOUIE BLUES

CROWN PUBLISHERS, INC., NEW YORK

Published by Crown Publishers, Inc., 201 East 50th Street, New York, New York 10022. Member of the Crown Publishing Group.

CROWN is a trademark of Crown Publishers, Inc.

Manufactured in the United States of America

Design by Shari DeMiskey

Library of Congress Cataloging-in-Publication Data

Tanner, Jake.
    Saint Louie blues / Jake Tanner.—1st ed.
    I. Title.
    PS3570.A553S25   1992   91-43632
    813'.54—dc20   CIP

ISBN 0-517-57675-9

10 9 8 7 6 5 4 3 2 1

First Edition

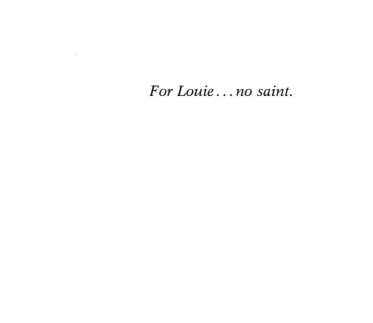

For Louie . . . no saint.

ACKNOWLEDGMENTS

My thanks to the following folks for their help in researching this book: Tom "Captain Amphetamine" Griffin, Colorado Bureau of Investigation; forensics mentor extraordinaire, Jack Swanburg, Arapahoe County Sheriff's Department Crime Lab; Doug and DoDo for the tour of Richmond; Gary Henderson, Associate Professor of Medical Pharmacology and Toxicology, University of California, Davis; Laura Watt, R.N., American Parkinson's Disease Information and Referral Center; . . . and Shela, the Irish nymph.

PROLOGUE

Car bomb, my ass! There was barely enough left of the DEA agent assembled on the slab to tell teeth from hemorrhoids. The whole thing had been a blind sider. I had just finished an energetic summer and it was my seventh day—autumn in Colorado. A time for contemplation and a lazy period in my life. I have a tough time lulling because of what inevitably follows. When I have a rare lull, the last thing I want to do is be confronted with graphic photos of the effects of explosives on the human form. I am rarely able to say no to trying to slap the hand of the outrageously asocial, even when it involves a pawn of the DEA. I guess I developed that sense in the police action that took a few years out of the prime of my life, and although the storm had arrived a bit too soon, it was an almost welcome hex.

He wasn't the first agent of the Drug Enforcement Agency of the Federal Bureau of Investigation within the Justice Department of the Federal Government of the United States of America who had landed on one coroner's slab or another just to be photographed by some callous forensic type. By the time some of them get there, it's hard to tell whose side they're on. Too many of them forget to separate role from reality. I have limited sympathy for the type. But it's not a job, it's an adventure, and if he didn't want to end up that way, then he shouldn't have signed up to be a *federale* who dealt with crazies in and out of his organization and his country.

If I hadn't been convinced that my destiny in life was to be a truth-and-justice hardass on strange battlefields, I probably could have stayed lazy in Colorado after the war. Worked on some dude ranch. Avoided the pictures. Ignored the implications. It never works out that way, somehow. I try to stay philosophical.

So this particular DEA agent was probably dead before he started because of the cross between his psychological profile and his career choice. I didn't have the time or the inclination to worry much about it. The first time I saw him, he was dead. I've never personally witnessed a resurrection. He stayed dead.

What I knew about him was what a pile of his disembodied parts looked like when the pathologist arranged them in some quasi-anatomically ordered manner for the fashion photographer from the crime files gazette. Didn't matter. He was just a piece of information at that point. There wasn't a goddamned thing I could do for him by then. I don't know whether he was solving the problem or was a part of the CIA distribution network. Good guy parts and bad guy parts look a lot alike.

Some bomb. The boob who made it should have stayed with the Irish Republican Army or the Palestine Liberation

Organization. They like to take out whole city blocks with their car bombs. Usually, when we say car bomb, we mean a neat little explosive designed to take an automobile and its occupants out of commission, not an entire vehicle full of explosives. It looked to me like the guy who smudged the DEA dude measured wrong. The neighbors were lucky they were out for the evening. Too bad there wasn't anything for them to come back to.

1

There are few brazen hardwoods in Colorado. In the fall, after God has finished painting the northeastern maples and the Midwestern oaks in brilliant oranges and reds, we get the only color left on the palette. The quaking aspen turns yellow.

I was born in Two Buttes on the eastern plains, but these days I spend my autumns in Coal Creek Canyon, thirty minutes from Denver, zoned mountain residential. There is a quirky charm to the season here. In the canyon, it's possible to waste an entire afternoon kicking back in a flannel shirt with your boots on a stump, watching the leaves chase each other around in the yard. In the absence of rain, I'm fond of chasing a crisp mountain breeze down the mountain on the motorcycle I keep around for just those occasions. There's a shrill excitement to it, snaking through the curves with the throaty engine throttled up and the vents in my leather jacket zippered against the promise of snow.

In the fall, Colorado can be a sunny seventy-five degrees one day and knee-deep in fresh powder the next. I remember the Halloween of '72. I spent the afternoon in the yard in shorts and a T-shirt planting bulbs for spring. I went into the house at five o'clock to fix supper and when I looked out again at seven, it was snowing. Eighteen inches by morning and drifts you could lose foreign cars in.

This year I'd started my fall preparations early. I had time on my hands and you never know whether autumn is going to last two months or two days. When winter comes, it comes. I hauled firewood under the eave so it would be good and dry by the time the first cold, snowy evenings arrived. Moved a couple of old cars back into the barn so they wouldn't get buried by snow and beat up by winter. That way I could sneak out and work on them occasionally with protection from the persistent wind. The upside of having antique-car restoration projects instead of cattle in your barn is that you never have to shovel out the cow chips.

I moved to Coal Creek after some lost years following a counterinsurgency engagement in southeast Asia. Originally I came here to see how drunk I could stay and how much I could forget of that nightmare called Vietnam. Eventually I sobered up and created just enough work for myself to feel marginally responsible. Fortunately, I had a bit of a nest egg from all the years when my generous salary and Caitlin's went straight into the bank. All expenses in those days were being paid through Rand by Uncle Sam. Then, too, the Company was pretty generous when she was killed. Caught in "friendly fire," they called it. I try to live off the returns, and everything is pretty much paid off, but when I get a wild hair that requires money, I usually need to scratch a little.

These days I like to think of myself as "B. F. Hopper, consulting investigator." I cleaned up my act a little since I first moved to Coal Creek. I've helped out some old buddies in law enforcement. Some of them had real tough cases and some were just running short on luck. Most of them know I'm bored with routine stuff, so they only call me when there's something particularly interesting cookin'. I don't mind. It's fun kicking a real bitch of a case around with an old friend. And I can usually bend the rules a bit more than they can. It's not big-time stuff, but at least the efforts in these little local wars seem to have a purpose.

I have also acquired other partners in this lifetime, or maybe they acquired me. They're more exigent and my assignments from them are always shaded toward the complex and dangerous. The assignment usually begins with a phone call from Stryker, and this one was no different.

Stryker Stephens is—pick one—a genius, a madman, a renegade, a scholar, a scientist, an expatriate, an ex-USAF intelligence officer, my mentor at the Rand Corporation during the Vietnam years, my trusted and loyal friend— all of the above.

As far as the world is concerned, Dr. Stephens is retired and owns a bar in Cabo San Lucas called the Two Yanks. Sometimes he's the bartender. Makes a mean margarita. The locals call him "Strai-care" and treat him like a respected Mafia don. For all the military mayhem and street violence that Stryker has been called upon to handle over the years, he is the most gentle man I know.

Right in the middle of my mellow Rocky Mountain autumn, the damned phone rang and rang and rang. I kicked back the screen door and strolled over to it, half-tempted not to answer. But then, it might be a damsel in distress wanting to feed me and tell me her problems. I don't mind solving those kinds of problems occasionally either.

"Hello."

"Hopper, are you alone?"

"Regrettably, Dr. Stephens, I am. Alone and singing the 'Ain't Had No Lovin' in a Long Time' blues. How are you?"

"In no mood for maudlin descriptions of your temporary celibacy. We have a problem of interest to the Foundation. It requires your services."

"Can it be discussed on this phone line?"

"Probably. However, I've sent you the background information via special courier. He should arrive within the hour. Stay off your motorcycle until he gets there. He also brings verbal instructions. Contact me this evening."

"Well, I suppose this is over and out, then."

"Correct."

A problem of interest to the Foundation. Translated that meant that someone was in the kind of trouble that required intervention by a cadre that could stretch the normal limits of the law. On behalf of a good guy or a good cause.

Some people are joiners. They belong to institutions. The military. A corporation. Club Med. The family business or the Kiwanis Club. Me? I break into a rash at the first hint of membership. So the only thing I belong to is this elitist clique named the Ki Foundation. And that was quite by accident.

The Foundation is a rubric that Stryker invented to get his missions accomplished. The whole team is only four people and a banker. And what a quintet it is.

In addition to Stryker the strategist and Hopper the operative, there's Lawless the lobbyist, Cordero the concierge, and Burroughs the banker.

Mike Lawless is probably Stryker's oldest friend and associate. He travels in the kind of Washington circles that most people only read about in the newspapers. He also travels in international circles that *nobody* ever reads about in anything. Elegant. Polished. And when we're in the same room, I always check for exits and never turn my back to him. Rumor has it that he's the second Yank. Dr. Stephens neither confirms nor denies that allegation.

Sergio Cordero is another matter. It's quite possible to mistake Sergio for the concierge of the Two Yanks. Stryker frequently has guests in Cabo who require unusual services—like private planes ready to fly to Bogota in the middle of the night. Sergio "arranges" such services. Truth is, Sergio is a good-looking kid from a rich Mexican oil family that educated him at UCLA and provided him with a wealth of diplomatic contacts. My first impression of him was as Stryker's sycophant. So much for first impressions. Cordero is an international entrepreneurial magician.

The Ki Foundation—that entity from which I was about to receive marching orders—might not have been created were it not for John Burroughs, our "silent" banker. Oh, we might have done some of the same things on a limited, informal basis because Stryker always has missions. Nevertheless, it's the nature of the credit line that John provided us that required a name and a tax-exempt corporate form.

As for John, he is the CEO of a very profitable holding company. Old Catholic money. We met because someone murdered his son and bureaucratic constraints on "the law" kept them from moving in on the perpetrator.

To the uninitiated, "Ki" sounds just like "key" and, in fact, the Key Foundation is the name that ended up on the credit line at John's friendly neighborhood bank in the Dutch Antilles. Although we've never talked about it, I know that Stryker intended "Ki," which in Southeast Asia means "invisible life force."

I heard several solid thumps on my front door. The courier was early.

2

ergio Cordero stood on my front porch looking like he'd prepared for an expedition to Antarctica. I don't know if anyone shares my perception, but I always think that Latins look very odd in heavy winter clothing. Despite the fact that it was still forty-five degrees in the mountains (which isn't considered cold here), Sergio was wearing a cashmere coat and was wrapped in a muffler that went around his heavy wool turtleneck sweater. The hands holding the briefcase were gloved in fleece-lined pigskin. To his credit, he was not wearing earmuffs or a cossack hat. His face was still the face that I am used to seeing in more tropical environs, the dark eyes set within features that are a subtle interplay between the Spaniard and the Mayan.

"Well, *muy buenas tardes, viejo.* Did you just decide to pay me a visit or are you the courier?"

Sergio smiled inscrutably. He has a hard time with my humor.

"*Puedo entrar,* Hopper, or are you going to make me stand out here like an errand boy?"

"*Pase y bienvenido a mi casa.* You've never been here before. I'll try to be a better host."

He walked into the entryway and I caught a glimpse of both of us in the mirror that hangs above the table that is home to my keys and stray pocket change. We could not be more different. When I stand next to Sergio, I look twice as tall as the six-foot-two that I am. Brown-blond hair, hazel eyes, and thrice his circumference in the chest. I look like an Oklahoma farm boy raised on ham and beans, bacon and eggs. He looks like a fashion model for menswear in La Prensa.

I saw him take the room in with a diplomat's lack of reaction. My home is done in American Male. Clean but cluttered with all the artifacts of unfinished tasks that are too boring to do like washing the dishes or putting the laundry away. Still, the massive stone fireplace is impressive and comforting and the wall of built-in bookcases, full to overflowing, speaks to other interests.

I took his coat and wondered what was so damned important that Stryker had felt compelled to send Sergio. He took the proffered cup of coffee. It was acceptable to him— a robust blend of three-fourths Tante Louise house and one-fourth espresso—good enough even for the Mexican coffee connoisseur. We settled ourselves into armchairs in the living room. I poured myself a Jack mist—an affectation I indulge in when I can get crushed ice to spit through the door of my space-age refrigerator. I poured Sergio a snifter of Armagnac from a squatty bottle with a crooked neck. If I surprised him, he didn't show it. He smiled one of those small contented smiles after the first swirl.

"I have very little time, Hopper. I have business at the Mexican Consulate before I return to the airport, and Stryker has requested some Maker's Mark and another small supply of Wolferman's muffins. All that before I return to your frenetic airport in a few hours. Why is it that you North Americans try to cram so many events into so little time and build everything so large and complex? It took me longer to get from your terminal to the car-rental lot than it takes me to get from the Los Cabos airport to Stryker's compound."

"Okay. You talk, I'll listen. What's this problem that is of such great interest to the Foundation?"

"Stryker received a call from an intermediary on behalf of a DEA insider. The contact said he was referred by Mike Lawless. Stryker confirmed it with Lawless first and then spoke again with the intermediary. This man was not willing to divulge the source of his information, but he said that the DEA lost an agent in Kansas City recently and that another DEA agent had been contacted by the Chief of Police from—how do you call it?—a 'backwater' town in Missouri. The Chief of Police furnished the DEA agent with some intriguing information."

"Lemme guess, Sergio. The DEA guy then went to his superiors and they were dead on their ass in terms of taking any action on the information from the backwater town. Am I close?"

He took a sniff and a sip of his Armagnac. The glass was already clouded with fingerprints from Sergio rolling the snifter in his hand while he contemplated his mission and his message.

"Not close, Hopper. Accurate. I think I have heard you say 'right on.' The contact knew of Lawless's relationship to Stryker, so he called. He cannot, of course, know of the

Foundation. But it seems an appropriate task for us since the Foundation is dedicated to helping people who have run out of options."

"How'd the DEA guy buy the farm?"

"Explosive dismemberment."

"One of the Kansas City 'families,' then."

"*Asi se hacen, los Sicilianos.* This is a part of the world that you know, yes? Kahnzas and Mizzuri?"

Sergio began to deliver the monologue that he was sent to deliver and I brought up my memories of Kansas and Missouri while I listened.

Indeed, it was a part of the world that I knew in at least two ways. My mother was born in what the locals would call "Kayansus," a pronunciation no better than Sergio's UCLA-groomed Mexican version, but more regionally authentic. She was one of thirteen children. Her nickname was Bummy, and before she met my rangy rancher father from Two Buttes, the person she was closest to in the whole world was my aunt Dodo. They were twins. Dodo and Bummy. The twins went to KC to train as nurses, which is where Mom met my dad. He had been kicked by one of the steers that he'd brought to show at the American Royal and showed up at the hospital where she was pulling her emergency-room training tour. There was a purity of spirit to my mother that was Midwestern wholesome, and that's the first way I got to know that part of the world. I listened to Sergio continue on one track while I reminisced on another. Another lesson from Stryker: There is no such thing as a one-track mind.

In later years, I became acquainted with the Kansas City mafia families. In the midst of corn, cattle, and Cadillac dealerships are operations involving drugs and prostitution that rival either coast in their perversity and their profusion. That's the second way I know that part of the world.

Sergio had talked for over an hour. I had touched up his Armagnac only once. He ended the monologue and reached for the briefcase. I winced.

"You know, my friend, our discussion has not made me happy. This already sounds like a bad 'Miami Vice' script. Drug czars have no rules anymore. Half the time you can't tell the white hats from the black hats. I've got no interest in bailing out the DEA. The DEA only exists as an apology for the politicians and the bankers who will sign off on pushers in schoolyards if it means that Third World countries can pay the interest on their Citicorp and Chase Manhattan loans with the proceeds from the sale of their dope. Damn, Sergio, have we decided to take this job?"

Sergio carefully extracted two inches of documents from his briefcase and laid them on my coffee table very slowly, very carefully. He looked me straight in the eye then, cool and appraising.

"I come from a culture too old and too Catholic to have such righteous or logical considerations, señor. I was born knowing the difference between supporting evil and making judicious deals with the devil on God's behalf. This is the rest of the information you need. My job here is finished for now."

Sergio downed the rest of his coffee, polished off his Armagnac, and stood. I gave him his coat, cursed the message that had just interrupted my autumn, and saw him to the door.

Sergio stopped bundling himself up for a moment. His posture was solemn.

"Stryker asks that you review the written material immediately. He asks further that you fly to the backwater town to make your own observations. He suggests the guise of a manufacturer who is seeking a new plant location. The relevant names have been researched by

Lawless's office and are included in the written material. Finally, he insists that you contact him this evening."

Sergio swept up the briefcase and exited before I could properly say good-bye. I had my marching orders and yet another perspective on the concierge.

3

he package of materials that Sergio left me included four documents and three eight-by-ten glossies. The first document was a confidential memo from the Police Chief to the DEA insider. The second document was the DEA guy's response and was marked FYEO. The third was the KCPD's file on the murder of the DEA agent, and the fourth was an editorial from the local newspaper in the backwater town. It was about the perils of drug abuse and it didn't say much except that the journalistic acumen of the local editorial staff was not high. The local rag opined that the federal campaign of "Just say no" was peachy keen. It was drivel.

The three glossies were in some ways more revealing.

There was a morgue shot of the DEA agent's parts being reassembled on the slab—far from sufficient to resemble the original man, but probably sufficient to suggest a protocol for pursuit of positive identification. There was enough metal mixed in to suggest that he might be part LTD.

The second glossy was an aerial photo of the backwater town with graphic outlines of probable industrial sites. It was information that supported Stryker's suggested cover.

The third photograph was of a woman.

This woman was reasonably attractive but somewhat . . . world weary, burdened. Odds on she was an informant, and I was to look for her.

Beyond that, I learned that Richmond, Missouri, was home to 5,499 people and the county seat of Ray County. The Police Chief was named Doug and the innuendo in his letter was that things smelled bad at City Hall. His grammar made me grimace, but the letter had the tone of a basically honest guy who still believed some of the stuff they told him at the big-city academy when he was a rookie. He named no names except the street names of the drugs involved. Besides the omnipresent heroin, crack, and cocaine, there were a few hot designer drugs that shouldn't have gotten to Missouri yet. He misspelled a fair number of them, erring on the side of the phonetic.

The Chief's argument to the DEA was that their dead agent had gotten too close to the connection between the K.C. families and his town. The letter was rather vague about what that connection might be. It had been typed on plain bond and remained unsigned. It was the kind of communication written by someone who might need, at a moment's notice, to deny that he'd written it at all.

The DEA's response was not exactly "Who gives a shit," but it wasn't encouraging. It referenced the difficulty that the DEA would have pulling someone off their "big" problems to respond to the death of one agent who may just have been in the wrong place at the wrong time. Ron Gable, the DEA agent to whom the letter was addressed, said he'd "check into it" with some "other contacts."

The KCPD report noted the possibility that the murder was a "gangland" killing, but the rest of it was pro forma.

So I had what amounted to ambiguous clues in a computer mystery game, but it was probably enough to start a discussion with Stryker. I needed to know a lot more about an intermediary who would take the time to pursue an issue that the DEA seemed to be backing off on. And I needed to know why the DEA was really backing off.

I dialed Cabo.

"Diga!"

Stryker always answers the phone as if he's half pissed off, just in case he doesn't want to talk to the person on the other end. I've learned to ignore or endure it, I'm not sure which.

"I'll ask you the same question I asked Cordero. Have we decided to take this one on?"

"You think we shouldn't?"

"Hold it, exalted one, I thought I was only an expendable operative. Besides, I only have one vote and far less than enough information to cast it."

"Hopper, if you're having a fit of pique because I didn't consult you more extensively at the beginning, then have it and call me back when you're ready to discuss the assignment."

"I'm not whining, Stryker. I just want to know what the point is. This stuff has been going on for years. Bad guys knock off DEA guys, half of whom pay for their vacations and kids' education selling drugs they confiscate. They've been working undercover so long they're indistinguishable from the real thing. Just seems to me that our talents might be better utilized elsewhere. Then I started to think about this intermediary that Sergio talked about. Who is he? Some old friend of Mike Lawless that we're doing a favor for?"

"You dislike Mike Lawless. That's acceptable. But it must not interfere in these situations."

"So answer the question."

"Ask it intelligently and I'll do my best."

"What am I really looking for?"

"The intermediary is not an old crony of Mike's. Mike, however, confirms that this messenger is credible. The man who took the trouble to call Mike believes that the K.C. families are using the Missouri town as a low-profile switching station for the underground rail system that distributes product to both coasts."

"Like hiding it in Telluride?"

"Yes, but more volume. And a sophisticated lab."

"So I'm on a fishing expedition?"

"So to speak. If there's nothing there, we'll drop it."

"All right. I'll leave tomorrow. Forgive me but I have to go turn myself into an enterprising industrialist. Do you want information on the cover?"

"Frankly, Hopper, I don't care what posture you adopt. Just get into all of the places you know how to get into. And report no less than once a week."

Stryker's the only man in the world who can tell me what to do and get away with it. And half the time I don't pay attention to him either. I hung up and went to the bedroom to look for business suits and a short-term identity.

4

I used to get to Kansas City by flying Frontier. I liked that a lot just because they had metal silverware, ceramic dishes, cloth napkins, and, occasionally, good food. Now it's either United or Continental—a pair of sixes. It's a two drink flight if you buy them both at the same time and don't let the Saran-wrapped ham and cheese croissant interrupt you for too long. That's another thing. Whatever happened to bread? Ham and cheese is supposed to be on rye, but I guess it's not trendy enough.

My ticket said that my destination was MCI. Kansas City has a hard time trying to figure out what they should call their airport. Signs leaving town call it KCI, and the OAG calls it MCI. MCI stands for Mid Continent International, probably because it's not near any major population center. It's so far from Kansas City that it's a wonder anyone even cares. Most folks who live there probably think it belongs to Lincoln, Nebraska, and drive to Topeka to start their vacations anyway.

MCI is one of the few airports in the world where you are just a few steps from your car when you disembark, but a half-an-hour bus ride away from an inter-airline plane change. I was ready for it.

I had decided not to engage in the extra layer of deception that's required if you're going to pretend you're from Chrysler or IBM. It would have meant printing a business card with a logo. Instead, I called a friend in Colorado Springs who now runs a successful high-tech shop with lots of defense contracts. He's a "brother" from the early seventies and knows how not to ask questions. I ended our phone call knowing the rudiments of what kind of site and security I would need for his kind of operation. At least enough to sell it to a Midwestern real-estate guy and the Chamber of Commerce if they had one.

A shuttle bus ride later, I was at the Hertz remote lot and in a dark metallic-blue Thunderbird so new that it still smelled funny. I had the car-rental map, which was about as helpful in this instance as the classified section of the *Tokyo Gazette*. The highway numbers that were in the real world weren't on the map and the highway numbers on the map didn't seem to exist in the real world. Neither did my destination. It was time to stop at my friendly neighborhood Texaco and *buy* a decent road map. You didn't used to have to do that.

The shortest way to Richmond is L. P. Cookingham Road or N.E. Cookingham Drive, depending on whether you believed the map or the road sign, to SH 291, to good ole Highway 69, thence to SH 10 and in. The most interesting way is to swing south on Interstate 435 to SH 210 and take it along the banks of the Missouri River. The interstate is like any other, built to military standards and about as exciting as a military fashion show. I elected the interstate to get me to the small towns along the river. It ran lazily through the undulating farmlands at the posted 55 MPH. Seems as if the Show Me State is still waiting for the news from Congress on the upgrade to 65. My T-bird did quite well at 70-plus.

Some of 435 is carved out of the rolling sandstone hills and some is on the flats, where you can see the old two-lane blacktop running parallel wherever the terrain took it. It was very cold for late fall by Midwestern standards and little patches of snow from a recent front were tucked behind every little hillock. The landmark for the exit is a water tower painted in Easter egg colors to look like a hot-air balloon. It matches the logo for Worlds of Fun, Kansas City's theme park. When I was growing up and would go to visit relatives in K.C., the amusement park was called Fairyland. When amusement parks gave way to theme parks, *that* park was on its way out. As you pass the park, the Kansas City skyline peeks up behind the crest of a hill. It's about the size of its Denver counterpart and serves as a signal to get off the interstate.

In spite of both the store-bought map and the Hertz map synopsis, SH 210 doesn't intersect with 435. Surprise. So off to the east along the valley of Missouri's Nile we go. I was in no great rush since I didn't have my heart in this one yet anyway. I decided to stop off at the Smuggler's Inn for a Jack. In and out . . . not exactly my kind of place, but you could feel comfortable taking your mother-in-law there. At least my blood-alcohol low light quit blinking.

As you leave the interstate to take the local route along the river, you pass through the expected river-bottom industrial areas. What you don't expect to see are the mammoth limestone/sandstone caves that warehouse megatons

21

of stuff that is part of the business of the Kansas City "U.S. Foreign Trade Zone," a neat gimmick to further screw up our balance of trade. I suspected that the uniqueness of this facility had not escaped the attention of the folks I had been sent by the Foundation to discourage.

It was rather ironic that the major named entity in the complex was "Hunt." There was more than enough activity at the zone to cover virtually any export/import activity, overt or covert. As I passed W. W. Granger and the Portland cement plant, a friendly sign informed me that it was a mere twenty-nine miles to the fair city of Richmond.

More industrial sites, a fireworks factory, a chemical company, and finally signs of rural commerce: hand-scrawled mini-billboards for potatoes and onions. At last the T-bird was in formation—the river, the railroad, and a three-tiered telephone pole squadron to the right and a single-tiered telephone pole unit to the left in a mile-wide river bottom.

The road is flat and straight between stretches where it chases itself around the terrain like it does in Coal Creek Canyon, different in that the trees alongside it are massive hardwoods. It chased me into Missouri City, population 404, where it becomes evident that the Bible Belt has staked out its claim on these parts. Signs read A GOING CHURCH FOR A COMING LORD and JESUS IS LORD, 1 MILE, then announce a stronghold of the ANCIENT FREE AND ACCEPTED MASONS. The town is run down and poor. The City Hall is located in a poorly maintained New England–style white frame church, discarded when the Missouri City Christian church moved into the brick and stained-glass facility next door. They ought to hope for a twister to wipe out the rest. Even at 25 MPH, the tour of Missouri City is over quickly.

I stopped in Orrick for a bottle of Jack and saw oak, ash, and hickory firewood for sale just past Creason's. Then I

cruised through the only four-way stop in Camden, population 219, where the stop signs still stand although the
electric stoplights have been shot out by a drunken farmer
mad at his banker. Only five more miles to Richmond.

My travel agent had booked me a room at the Rose Court.
She said it was the only one listed in the Red Book for
Richmond. I was thinking of selecting a major moderate
chain—like the one that always keeps its porch light burning—to maintain a conservative image. Until you hit the
Fortune 500, manufacturing types are usually not high-
rollers. They stay at medium-priced hotels and eat at
medium-priced restaurants unless they're courting a customer. It appeared that I wasn't going to have to make
any of those decisions at my intended destination.

Richmond is like any other town that time has forgotten.
It has a bar or two, a Walmart, a central square with a
typical court house, signs for the meeting places of the
Rotary, Kiwanis, and other civic clubs, some wonderful
old homes, some tract houses, some trucks, some rednecks,
a diner or two, and one damned motel.

Richmond was platted in 1827 as a county seat and
incorporated in 1835. It was on the road west, a trail that
hooked up with the much more famous trails like the Santa
Fe, which runs through a suburb of Kansas City, and the
old Shawnee Mission. It was a border town during the
Civil War with sympathizers for both the Union and Confederate causes. Richmond is the final resting place of
Bloody Bill Anderson, an infamous bushwhacker who rode
with Quantrell, and Bob Ford, the man who shot Jesse
James.

Before the Civil War, Richmond played a part in the
"Mormon War," and today a statue of Colonel Alexander
Doniphan stands in the town square. Doniphan distin-
guished himself as the leader of a Missouri regiment in the
Mexican War and later defied the order of a superior officer

23

who wanted him to shoot Joseph Smith, founder of the Mormon Church. After the war, Richmond became the center of a major coal-mining region, an era that ended with World War I. Richmond has a lot of history and not many people. Like every other small town in America, it has financial problems and no assurance of survival in an economic climate that favors large metropolitan areas and is killing the independent farmer.

I had a choice of tactics. I could broadside these folks with an aggressive presence, or I could sort of slide into the community sideways with someone local acting as my representative. Anyone who's ever been a part of a Midwestern small town knows that locals don't take kindly to being broadsided. The only folks you can find as representatives in a small town are people who stand to make some money from representing you. Real-estate brokers—pick a Rotarian or a J.C.—generally work just fine. They'll lunch and dinner you to death with just about anyone you want to meet because they envision commissions bulging in their cowhide tri-folds.

There are no Coldwell Bankers in Richmond. I checked for a Chamber. The Chamber of Commerce is on the north side of the square in the Farm Bureau Building, which a placard said was given to the Boy Scouts of Richmond by William F. Yates in memory of his parents in 1957. The Chamber is in a small office in the back of the first floor. A nice young lady from another office came in to tell me that the Chamber maid was out for a while. She asked if she could help. When I told her what it was I needed, she said that because of Chamber policy she wasn't in a position to recommend any single person, but that she could give me the names of the Chamber members who specialized in commercial real estate. There were only two. She hesitated on the second. I got the name of Roscoe E. Morton III as the expert on industrial property. I made the call. And I'll be damned if it wasn't a Century 21.

Thirty acres, I said. Not a dime more than a buck seventy cents a square foot. Ten percent commission, said Roscoe. Maybe seven, I said. That was over $150K and more money than Roscoe had seen in a few years. We were in business.

To his credit he asked the right questions and made the right suggestions. We made an appointment for breakfast. I slept well that first night. The next morning I showered, dressed, and hit Ethridges on the north side of the courthouse right on schedule.

Ethridges has a fake brick front with pressed metal trim on the second story. The black awning over the door is emblazoned with a calligraphed *D*. God knows why. Two panels announce the hours of operation, and they even agree with each other. The Richmond R-16 school district wrestling schedule was posted on the right and the soup of the day was navy bean. I put on my Farber face.

Roscoe E. Morton III was a product of the times. Not a bad guy, just an opportunistic one. He was waiting for me by the cashier's station just inside the second door. His uniform was a gold Century 21 blazer with enough lapel pins to decorate a general, a light yellow button-down oxford cloth shirt, brown and gold plaid tie, off-gray/tan slacks, and cordovan tassle loafers. The Missouri version of "dress for success" was enough to make you weep, but his eyes were intelligent and we were about to dance.

"Good to see you, Mr. Ferber."

"That's Farber. Jim Farber. Let's get a table."

Ethridges was deeper than it was wide, with large tables and high-back Early American chairs in the center. The booths were green. The backs were plaid. The benches solid. They were dressed in custom-fitted orange vinyl table covers. There was even more orange on the walls. Each table had a hurricane oil lamp. Roscoe clashed with the decor.

The place was warm and hometown. An attractive petite waitress with shoulder-length light brown hair sat us at a booth along one side of the place and out of the traffic. As she handed us the menus, I noticed her deep blue eyes, and as she turned to get us our coffee, I was distracted momentarily by the rest of her assets. The guy at the next table called her Connie when he asked about an error on his check. She just winked at him and told him to change it himself. Said she always could talk better than she could add. Roscoe put his menu aside while I searched mine for biscuits and country gravy.

"Great buns here, huh?" He winked a good-ole-boy conspiratorial wink.

"Hmmmm . . ."

"So as I understand it, Mr. Farber—"

"Jim. Please."

" . . . You're looking for an industrial site in these parts. It's a smart move. We may not have the population of Metro Kansas City or the industrial intensity of North Kansas City, but we've got the work force. We've got a lot more hard-workin' blue-collar rednecks than people of color, if y'know what I mean. And we've got the prettiest little town in Missourah. A proud place for any family to raise their kids in."

I looked up from the menu and glared at him. Subtly.

"Just get me maintained streets, rubbish removal, water, electricity, gas, and sewer to the property line plus a city government that's going to appreciate a hundred and fifty new jobs. More than an additional fifty the next year. Get me results without red tape. I need a site and some introductions."

Roscoe took the opportunity to smile up at the pixie who was pouring us each a cup of coffee, but he'd heard me. We went into round two.

"Who do you need to see, Jim? You call it. I can only think of three sites the size that you need. I control 'em, but one of 'em belongs to a real tough trader. In spite of the ownership, I think that particular one is perfect and we could make the other two happen. I certainly do want to work with you because I know I can make you the best deal you can find in this area. I've lived in Ray County all my life. Just tell me what you need to know."

Roscoe Morton used to play football; he had a fast practiced line and knew all the plays, although he had forgotten where to carry his weight. His hair was styled the way he'd probably worn it when he was in high school—in a swept-back pompadour now exposing a more accentuated widow's peak, with no part. He had a cherubic baby face and some of his breakfast still hung on his plaid rayon tie. His eyes were a little watery and he ate with the weight of his upper body supported by his elbows on the table, but I was beginning to like him anyway.

"Well, Roscoe, let's just stop being good old boys, whaddya say? I need a site that isn't going to have any problems with the people who issue permits, and I'm going to need a Mayor who can tolerate a high-security manufacturing facility in his town. I also need a chief of police who can walk and chew gum at the same time so I can hire some cops to cover the security on weekends. You got or not?"

"I got. Spend three days with me."

"I got two days."

"All right. We'll do it in two days, pardner."

5

We developed an eccentric relationship, Roscoe and I. Productive but eccentric. He pushed away half-eaten hotcakes and pulled out his maps to show me three parcels. The industrial park fit my specs, the site by the candy factory could have worked as well, but one of them intrigued me. It was a ranch on the far north side of town with good access but lots of privacy. Roscoe said the owner was a farm implements guy whose family had had the only International Harvester distributorship in the area for over thirty years.

"Now, there's no way that ole Jack Casey is hurting, y'understand. That's real old money. But with agribusiness going to hell in a handbasket and I.H. havin' its own hard times, I believe I could get Jack motivated to sell you a piece on the frontage road. It's about a mile from the home place."

"Is his family going to mind having a factory that makes missile parts in its front yard?"

"Aw, hell no. Casey's a businessman. Worst that could happen to you is he'll try to sell you his nephew as a vice-president or somethin'." Roscoe paused and rolled his eyes, which was all I needed to know about the nephew. Then he leaned forward conspiratorially.

"Missile parts, huh? Guv'mint contracts and such?"

"Yessir. This is an expansion plant. We're headquartered in Colorado Springs near the Consolidated Space Operations Center."

I had my friend in the Springs standing by to verify my identity in case someone wanted to check. Whoever it was, it wouldn't be Roscoe. Roscoe was busy thinking about how much hay he could make with Casey by bringing him a buyer like me. I had my representative just where I wanted him—dreaming of crisp new C notes stuffed in his Levi's.

"Well, I'll set up a time with Casey to show you around tomorrow morning. Do you want to see the other two pieces?"

"Not just yet. And before I see Casey, I have some other research to do. I've got five key people to move to this new plant and they've got wives and families who are picky about their living environment. I need to know something about this town. I'm going to spend the rest of the morning just roaming around. Without you. Besides that, there's the matter of security that we talked about. Who's your Police Chief?"

"Guy by the name of Doug Ketchum. A lot of the law-enforcement folks hereabouts are local football heroes back from tours as MPs. Not Doug. He's a pro. Graduated from his first law-enforcement academy in 'sixty-eight and the FBI National Academy in 'seventy-nine. We were real lucky to lure him here from the big city. You'll like him. He's a good man."

I snorted. "Ketchum? What the hell kind of name is that for a cop? Oh, well, I guess none of us gets to choose. Can you set something up with him and maybe the City Manager or whoever it is that really runs the place?"

"No problem. Mayor's office hours are three to five-thirty, and I think I can get Doug and Shelley from the Chamber of Commerce there, too. You sure you don't want any company on your tour?"

It was almost noon and I was restless.

"I'm sure, Roscoe. You're just going to have to trust this little town of yours to show well all by its ownself."

"Well, come on to the car with me and I'll show you where City Hall is at least. I'll meet you there at four-thirty. Here's my card if you need to get a hold of me before then."

Roscoe paid for breakfast at the cash register near the front door and we turned to go. A woman opened the door of the café, and despite the fact that her makeup was laid on a bit too thick for me, I knew that I was looking at the girl from the eight-by-ten glossy. Long auburn hair and green eyes. Her legs took up two-thirds of the space between her ankles and her ears. Just the way I like 'em. She was prettier in person than in the photo, with a lot of potential underneath the foundation and mascara. But for now she was just part of the puzzle and I instructed my gonads to take five.

She nodded to my companion.

"Howdy, Roscoe."

"Mornin', Mimi. Just getting off work?" Roscoe leered. She was up to it. Mimi just walked up and pinched his cheek.

"That's what I like about you, Roscoe. You're such a smart ass." She swayed nicely on her way to the table. I never will figure out how some women walk that way without throwing something out of whack. We stepped outside.

"Who's that?"

"Aw, that's just Mimi. Every town has one. A round heels who sometimes does it for money and sometimes for love. When her bank account gets too low, she does it for money and Doug's boys have to pick her up every once in a while. We're right smack in the middle of the Bible Belt, ya know. She's always out the next day. No big deal."

He pointed out City Hall, the police station, fire department, and city maintenance complex on the map and left me standing on the sidewalk. I was tempted to walk back into the café, but I had other fish to fry.

6

I walked around like a tourist in the beginning, spending a good bit of time in the town square reading the legends on the statues of the fallen heroes of Richmond. All four sides of the courthouse have the inscription "Obedience to the Law Is Liberty" in that too often used Roman lettering. Colonel Doniphan's statue is on the west courthouse lawn. He died in Richmond in 1887. The plaques on the statue extol his many virtues, including his "immense stature," "brilliant parts," and "eloquence beyond description." Sounds a little like the Second Coming.

I went inside the courthouse to see if I could find a county road map and a telephone book. Winter's eve and the lack of a basement was announced by the snow blowers parked in one wing of the plus-sign-shaped lobby. A fallout shelter sign and an arrow pointed the way to the second floor. I decided to try there for the map. Bingo. Map in hand, I continued my tour after a short pause for the cause, during which I found the lawnmowers stashed in the men's room leaking oil on a flattened cardboard box. I left by the east door, past the lazy pendulum ticks of the grandmother clock on the wall.

The east lawn has a statue in memory of Donald Louck erected courtesy of the American Legion Griffith Post #237 and a small replica of the Vietnam War Memorial in Washington. It was the only asymmetrical thing on the square, a double entendre.

The square is pretty typical of small-town America with the usual storefront shops—a paint store, a TV repairshop, a leather shop, a carpet store, a men's clothing store, a florist, a jeweler, and an Economy Drug variety store. Nearly anywhere you look you can see a financial institution of some sort, Boatman's Bank among them. Insurance offices, accountants' offices, and farm-credit bureaus crop up here and there. Stroebel's New York Life office says it's been serving Ray County since 1877—maybe that's why there's a turtle in the window. A quilt store makes it rural. A storefront Baptist church makes it Bible Belt and partly black. An empty storefront makes it economically depressed like much of the rest of the country. A dentist and a barber make it homey. Scattered lawyers' offices and a title insurance office make it the county seat.

On the northeast corner is a funeral home, where I'm told the proprietor also graciously serves the county as coroner. The public-service company has an office to help them collect bills right next to Stanley's Gym, where weights and boxing seem to have given way to aerobics classes. Today's class has a shapely member or two, and I try not to leave my noseprint on the window.

One office stood out among the others on the square. It was a dark red brick renovation with an architect's touch, which included a handsome glass-block and brick entryway. Everyone in Richmond was not economically disenfranchised. The brass sign on the side of the entry said LAVELLE AND ASSOCIATES, ATTORNEYS AT LAW.

I chatted with clerks in small stores, where I went to buy corn nuts and pork rinds. I went to the Ray County Museum, where the caretaker took me through the life of the area and pointed me to the stacks of back issues of the Richmond newspapers and court records that I would never read. I learned about all the wars, the Mormons, coal mining, and agriculture.

While I was driving around, I saw federally subsidized housing projects, HUD rentals, derelict antebellum homes, renovated Victorian beauties, tract houses, farms, and giant new castle monuments to the few moneyed who had elected for some reason to stay in Richmond. I drove up a hill to the water tower to find modest homes over the ridge. I drove up another hill north of town to find the high-rent district. Generally, though, the houses were scattered about town, big next to small, new next to old, trashed-out next to trim, with no clear master plan in evidence. I returned to the square.

Well, as they say on the old TV cops-and-robbers shows, I had cased the joint. New York it wasn't. As in most other small towns, the only thing that counted was the way the people were put together. Nobody runs New York City or Washington, D.C., or Chicago, although some might think they do. But somebody always runs a town like Richmond. It was almost four-thirty. Show time. I headed for City Hall.

Roscoe was waiting for me on the steps under one of those off-white corrugated fiberglass awnings. The City Hall looked as if it might have been a school at one time, red-brick war-era architecture. About half of the windows had the awnings, and a couple were sprouting air-conditioning units. Four of the windows at one end looked as if they had been bricked up with fire-sale beige brick, probably by the low bidder or a past mayoral nephew.

Roscoe opened the door for me and led me up a flight of stairs that had seen better days, then down a short hallway and into the Council chambers. A sign taped to the beaded glass in the door said QUIET PLEASE in green Magic Marker. The room was furnished like a bad Jimmy Cagney movie. Some furniture manufacturer had locked up the Mid-western government markets in the early forties, and the uncomfortable wooden chairs are getting to be de facto antiques. There were a couple of those left and a hodge-podge of everything from plastic-covered swivel desk chairs to the folding high-school auditorium type. Two tables were set in a "T" behind a low courtroom-type room divider with a swinging barroom door. There were three old church pews for the audience set on unpainted ply-wood risers. The white guest lectern looked like a school shop project.

On the wall at the head of the table was an Oriental-style loop rug, probably made by the local DAR, with an eagle holding a banner in its beak that proclaimed "1776–1976." I wondered what had been there before 1976. An American flag was tucked stage left and a mystery flag stage right. The bricked-up windows I had seen from the outside were behind the pews. The room was paneled with cash-and-carry printed vinyl pressboard. On the wall opposite the windows was the zoning map thumbtacked on a four-by-six sheet of white garbage board. It was covered with clear plastic, which showed many moons of leftover grease-pencil tracks.

There were three people already in the room—a man, a broad, and a cop. Bets that the cop was the Chief. White

35

male. Last Name: Ketchum—King, Edward, Tom, Charlie, Henry, Union, Mary. First Name: Douglas—common spelling. Middle Name: Don. DOB: two, twenty-five of forty-four, five-eight, 155, blue and blond.

The guy seated at the center of the top of the "T" sure looked like a mayor to me. Early fifties, nearly bald with the rest pasted back except for an unruly fringe over his large ears. He absently smoothed what little there was with his hand. His ears held up black horn-rimmed glasses over the top of which bushy eyebrows escaped. He had a pasty pink complexion and hairy arms which hung out of a yellow sport shirt with maroon buttons. He stuck one of them out at me. I didn't like his handshake and I didn't like his eyes, but he hardly looked like one of the corrupt small-town Bible Belt mayors of yore. Roscoe introduced him as Bill McCain.

"How do you do, Mr. Farber. Roscoe tells me you're thinking of bringing some development to our fair town. We'd like to make sure you get the information you need. This is Doug Ketchum, our Chief of Police, and right next to him is Shelley Stone, who's just about the entire staff of the Chamber of Commerce. Have a seat."

I nodded to Morton, who looked alert and a little uncomfortable. Shelley Stone was flashing me a Pepsodent smile and she looked more like a Welcome Wagon lady than a Chamber of Commerce type. In Denver, the Chamber of Commerce people wear three-piece suits and speak like the corporate executives they are trying to recruit. Her plaid A-line skirt and fluffy blouse might not have suited Denver, but it looked damned good in Richmond. The Chief had the dispatcher/girl Friday bring coffee up from the squad room in the basement. The Mayor waited until she left and then reached into a beat-up scissor-top leather briefcase.

"Now, Doug, if you'll just take a short duty break. I'm going to see if this fellow will share some sour mash. I never did like that Carrie Nation ordinance. It's un-American."

With that he placed a fine old bottle of Kentucky sour mash in front of me. I didn't mind. Didn't look to me like Doug minded much either, although he and Shelley abstained. Roscoe, McCain, and I sipped the sour mash from Styrofoam cups, even though good whiskey deserves heavy-bottomed tumblers. On the other hand, the Styrofoam didn't affect the taste much and this whiskey was the top of the line.

I watched the Mayor for signs that the preamble was over. He said a couple more inconsequential things and then leaned back in his chair. I took the opportunity to appreciate the delicate curve of Shelley's neck. She was the kind of woman who had all the equipment to drive most men crazy, probably made her husband happy some of the time, and didn't allow anyone else to make her happy at all. I damn sure wouldn't have minded trying but suspected that that might be out of the question. Back to work.

"So what questions can we answer for you, Jim?" said the Mayor.

"Well, I think Roscoe has a leg up on the real estate, so I'm more interested in talking with you about the kinds of services that are available in this town. You see, I have a two-part problem. First, I've got some managers to relocate and they're going to want to know about schools, hospitals, shopping, all of that. Second, we have a security-sensitive business. I'll build all the security bells and whistles into the plant, but industrial espionage is common practice in my business and sometimes I have to base site selection on the cooperation of local law enforcement. I suspect Shelley here can tell me about the quality-of-life issues"—I smiled at her disarmingly because I had a role for her to play later—"but for now I'd like to tell you what I need in the way of backup for my security system."

Doug leaned forward. One eyebrow was arched over a

tan and weathered leathery face. His uniform with its gold Chief's badge was crisp right down to the spit-polished plain-toe oxfords. He looked interested. This was clearly a less boring problem than breaking up bar fights and locking up the drunks on weekends. Shelley looked a little disappointed that she couldn't do her booster speech and the Mayor stared into his sour mash. I continued.

"Doug, in Colorado Springs the Police Chief has created a detail of investigators who are specialists in high-tech security. Now, the Springs is an aerospace and military town and I'm not expecting that here. But I've got to have a couple of guys in your outfit who'll be interested in working with us. Preferably young and preferably bright. A rigid military background wouldn't hurt. I'll get the Chief in the Springs to send one of his guys out to do a little training if that would be acceptable to you. You got anybody like that?"

Doug started to answer, but the Mayor preempted him.

"I don't think you want any of the young guys. We got a guy who used to be the Police Chief in this town, and I think he could probably take care of you just fine as an independent. He works real well with Doug's men. Name of Luther Brock. What do you think, Doug?"

So the very first thing of importance that I learned in Council chambers was that the Police Chief couldn't stand the Mayor's guts. I learned it only because I was watching Doug's eyes and the set of his jaw. That's where you look for rage in the overcontrolled cop types. I found it in spades. Just a little narrowing of the lids and a tightening of the internal pterygoid muscles of the jaw. It was all I needed. When Stryker was training the counterinsurgence crew at Rand, he spent one whole week making us memorize the muscles of the face and neck. He used to bark at us a lot. "Forget all that crap about the eyes being the window to the soul. In point of fact, the muscles of the face

38

are the window to the ego and the body's intention. Learn to read them. It will save your life someday."

He turned out to be right about that. For the moment, the technique was also giving me my first clues about the underbelly of the situation.

Doug handled it diplomatically.

"We could probly work somethin' out with Luther. There's a coupla other guys who might be interested, too. I think we can handle it. Just what is it you're wantin' to make at the new plant?"

I had my product information ready and Doug nodded as if he knew what I was talking about, but I knew it was Greek to everybody but me. When I mentioned Department of Defense contracts, the Mayor stirred again. He had a way of wrinkling his brow when he was interested in something. His voice was big and low.

"Does that mean we're going to be overrun with federal types, Jim? How often do they come and check up on you?"

His smile was a tiny bit strained and that gave me my second piece of useful information. For some reason, the Mayor was concerned about any federal presence in his sleepy little burg. It was a ridiculous concern since the quality-control inspectors and contracts administrators from DOD are not looking for spies or bad guys, they're looking for parts. Occasionally a security review will bring in a fed fuzz or two. Mostly administrative types instead of Dick Tracys. Or the feds would put Richmond on the tour simply to add a day of fishing to their itinerary.

I decided to zing him a little just to see what I'd get.

"Federal inspectors show up once or twice during the life of a contract. I don't think you can call it being overrun. You got something against the feds, Mayor McCain?"

Old Bill raised his hands, palms toward me and open as if to say "Who, me?"

"Not at all, Jim, and fact is, we'd welcome the business.

39

This is a decent town and we support the U.S. Government in every way we can. I guess I just don't like bureaucrats, other than homegrown, that is. You know the other kind. The ones who come in with six inches of laws that tie a businessman's hands. Are you gonna need anything in the way of special permits for pollution or hazardous waste, that kind of thing?"

"Usually we don't. I'll let the Government Relations Department figure that out with the state and federal agencies. Am I gonna have any trouble with a building permit for eighty thousand square feet?"

"Lord no, boy. Roscoe here says that you're lookin' to buy thirty acres. Why so much if you only want to build eighty thousand square feet?"

"Corporate policy. We set back at least two acres around the perimeter and we have other outbuildings. Is there anything in your city code that prevents me from building a twenty-foot fence around the facility?"

Roscoe piped up.

"I think we can handle the height restrictions, Jim."

I turned to Shelley, who was still concentrating on looking sprightly. Fifteen minutes later I knew everything I needed to know about the new shopping mall, the Iowa test scores from the school system, and the annual Mushroom Festival—in honor of the annual crop of wild morel mushrooms.

I played my last card. The Mayor was busy sneaking more sour mash into his cup, and Doug was pretending to listen to Shelley as if he hadn't ever heard her pitch before.

"So, Shelley, one of the first things the wives of my management team are going to ask about is drugs in the schools. A lot of them have teenaged kids and they worry about stuff like that. I'd also like your view of it, Doug."

Well, Shelley just launched. The woman had a whole lot of opinions. She enthusiastically told me that she had personally started a community committee against drugs. She became the PTA-loving, Sunday school–teaching, family-rearing, faithful, straight, small-town housewife and community leader that she was. What a waste. She rattled on. I caught the slight movement of both eyebrows on the Mayor and the sudden tension in Doug's body.

I let Shelley finish. It was textbook American apple pie. Time to close this one up. Besides, it looked as though the Mayor was through sharing his bourbon.

"Thank you, Shelley. I'm certainly pleased to see that this town is so motivated about the issue."

I turned to the congregation.

"Well, folks, I certainly appreciate your taking the time to speak with me. Roscoe and I are going to start dealing with landowners in the morning. Mayor McCain, I'd like to talk with you further about what you see as the most likely economic future of your town. We like to locate in places that are still small enough to provide us room to grow, but we want a location that can support our kind of operation. I'll get back to you after I know whether I can make a deal on some dirt."

"Roscoe tells me you're looking at the Casey piece. Good man, Jack Casey."

"Roscoe tells me he's a tough trader."

The Mayor guffawed and somehow it seemed inappropriate. "He's tougher than most, I guess, but he's not impossible. Best of luck to you."

"Thanks for your hospitality." I raised my Styrofoam cup to McCain and his little fiefdom. He bowed with noblesse oblige, then walked out. Shelley said her good-byes and announced that she'd be pleased as punch to speak with any of my mythical management wives.

I made a date with Roscoe to see Casey at eleven o'clock the next morning. He left next. Finally, it was just me and the Chief. He wasn't moving. I decided I'd lead.

"Doug, you know you can't get into much detail at meetings like these. If you're off duty, I'd like to buy you a beer and pick your brain some more."

He looked at me as if he was pleased to be asked, and I realized suddenly how young he was. Young but savvy. So dry behind the ears that even a mosquito would be uncomfortable there. It was too soon to gauge his level of ambition, but it couldn't have been easy being the Chief in a small town where the Mayor called your shots.

"Sure. No problem. There's a pretty good bar across the street from the courthouse, name of Ethridges. Or you can wait till I get out of this uniform and I can have more than a cup at a little place out in the country."

I told him I still had a few things to do and I knew where Ethridges was. The average observer would not have sensed his preference for the civvies and the out-of-town bar, but there would be plenty of time for that in the days to come. We drove separate cars, met at the bar, and settled into a booth. I ordered a draw and he ordered a coffee, black. The few who found their way to the bar in this upstanding town nodded or said howdy to the Chief.

The bar was just off to the left as you entered, past a small anteroom that housed the cigarette machine. A Rock-ola jukebox that looked like a home-stereo console was at the far end. The underside of it, which you could see when you raised the top to make selections, looked like a comfortable old oil painting. The back bar was a warehouse of glasses of all the traditional types and sizes racked up on glass shelves. Off the near end of the bar there were two small tables and the booth we had settled into. There were only five black vinyl bucket-seated bar stools at the black vinyl padded rail. The orange wall-covering motif of the main room in Ethridges continued here above the two four-person booths across from the bar, and displayed the historical drawings I had seen earlier at the Ray

County Museum: a coal mine, a thrashing machine, an old iron-lattice bridge across the river, and the courthouse. A Beefeater statue stood guard over a Matilda Bay Cooler box on the back-bar wall.

"Your Mayor sounded like he was trying to fix this job for his old pal Brock. I don't like mayors much, Doug. I'd rather hear what you have to say."

The small-town reserve stayed firmly in place.

"Oh, Luther's not bad. Like Bill says, he's been around the block a few times. Trouble is, he's not a technical guy. I hired me a young kid who's pretty sharp at computers. He'd probably understand the high-tech shit a lot better than Brock."

"You call it. I don't let mayors make security decisions for me."

"Well, this Mayor don't always make the decisions you want him to make from a law-enforcement point of view. I guess that's true of any town, though."

"Born here?"

"No, but my in-laws go back to when they settled it. Think they must have come over as part of the Mormon invasion. What about you?"

"Born in Colorado. But my mother's from Ottawa, Kansas, a little south and just over the line."

With that credential established, I went on to ask innocuous questions about the size of his department and whether he allowed moonlighting. I maneuvered my way back to Shelley.

"That Chamber of Commerce lady is sure a talker."

Doug snorted. "Shelley? Shelley's a well-meaning lady, but you have to take most of what she says with a grain of salt."

"Was she bullshitting me about drugs in the schools?"

"Yeah. Her speech came right out of the League of Women Voters briefing paper. We got a whole passel of righteous churchgoers who think they can teach everybody to just say no. Don't get me wrong. Our problem isn't any worse than any other community our size. Problem is there's too much trouble our kids can get into in K.C. And we got some bikers who don't help much either. Can't say the local bench is much help to us. Judge Gaiters makes some calls that don't seem so supportive of local police efforts. Kinda like McCain. But let me turn the tables on you, Jim. Are you bringing a bunch of yuppie snorters into my town?"

"No way. We've been doing voluntary drug testing for years. You wanna work for us, you volunteer. I can't afford to have anyone make the kind of mistakes that get made when your labor force is fucked up on one thing or another."

We commiserated for a couple of minutes and I polished off my draw. I took my leave and promised to get back to him if we made the decision to relocate. He shrugged as if that wouldn't make his life any easier, but it wouldn't make it any harder either.

I headed east out of town on SH 10, a mildly winding two-lane where the T-bird became a fun toy. Excelsior Springs was just seventeen miles up the road, and I had remembered the Elms from a former lifetime. It was an old resort hotel with some wonderful amenities. I'd be damned if I was going to stay in the Rose Court, Richmond's only, and stand in the parking lot to make semi-impossible phone calls to Mexico.

7

Fall in Missouri is a lot different than it is in Colorado. I rolled my window down and smelled the early evening. Pollution isn't an issue in rural America yet, and the smell of burning leaves took me back to a time when you just raked 'em to the curb and torched 'em. I had forgotten how brilliant the maple leaves got, especially after a wet summer. I let digital search find WDAF 61 Country and Dan Diamond on the T-bird's command-center console and was rewarded with K. T. Oslin's "80's Ladies." She got to the refrain about "There ain't much these ladies ain't tried," and I thought about Mimi. She looked like the type that didn't have much left to try... or to lose, for that matter.

I was just squeaking through one of the tighter turns when I saw a sight that makes some people's hearts stop. Junction of 10 and N. A biker bar. A mostly Harley/lots of chopper/even distribution of Confederate flags and American flags/Maltese cross/down-and-dirty biker bar. You can tell them by the fact that the damned bikes are always backed into formation in the front and the license plates are all local. If you're not a biker, you're not likely to feel too welcome there. It's not that bikers are always and necessarily bad news. It's just that when they get drunk or drugged up—or just plain feel like it—they can be nasty and unpredictable.

There are two things you never do in that kind of bar. First, you never flirt with a biker chick, even if she's coming on to you. You make friends with her old man and you wait—he'll probably loan her to you. Second, you never ask questions about anything but their scooters till they let you inside the circle. I like bikers because they're loyal, and once you're in, you're in. Besides, I can talk motorcycles all night long and have been reported to be a little unpredictable myself. Have a good time doing it, too. I would have stopped to check this one out, but I wasn't dressed right.

I checked into my room at the Elms. The Elms, in addition to its new godawful disco bar, has a quiet bar along one wall of the restaurant and a good trolling bar in the lobby. The inn was originally completed in July of 1888 but burned down only ten years later. The second building registered its first guests on July 24, 1909, and also burned to the ground—one in the morning, Sunday, October 30, 1910. Not to be denied, persistent mineral-water lovers built yet a third, which stands today. The formal opening was September 7, 1912. It was built without a disco or the New Leaf Spa with its environmental rooms like the Polynesian, African, Oriental, French, and Roman. I wonder why they left out the Greeks. They'd never get away with that in San Francisco. I plopped onto a bar stool in the lobby bar and ordered a double Bombay, rocks.

I was at that irritating point in a field investigation where I had enough suspicion to keep me motivated but not enough data to get moving in any specific direction. I could only verify some of Doug's letter to the federal agency. Something smelled of decay in Richmond, but so far I had no evidence that it was anything more than his sour grapes about the lack of support coming from City Hall. Except for the DEA agent who bought the farm.

That was intriguing. It was not a mild murder. There wasn't enough of him left to make a McDonald's quarter-pounder. I couldn't ignore it.

Bottoms up. To room. I'm fond of simple tasks at that time of day.

I was restless and checked my suitcase for more casual threads. I grabbed my button-fly Levi's, a wool plaid shirt, and some roughout shitkicker boots and went off to look for a burger. I opted for the biker bar so I could take care of my appetite and my curiosity at the same time.

In Colorado, the bars that don't want bikers, or at least don't want bikers who look like bikers, post signs that say "no colors." The bars that like bikers make sure they have plenty of cold beer, bullet-proof furniture, an ability to see no evil, and tough tunes on the jukebox. "Born to Be Wild" is over twenty years old, but bikers still play it like it was their national anthem.

I smelled the bar three steps before I opened the door. Years of tobacco smoke and spilled beers soak into the old wood-plank floors and marinate them forever. You usually can't smell the bikers until you're sitting next to them at the bar, and after a while you get to the point where you can't smell anything at all.

The door was red and it was on the side of a long, narrow,

gray-stucco cinder-block building with a battered canvas awning. I was relieved to hear the hiss of meat on a grill accompanied by the smell of frying onions. God knows whether I'd get any information, but I was damned sure going to get my burger.

I took the room in all at once. The bar was to the left and dog-legged from the door, running almost to the front of the room before it curved back to the wall. It left just enough room at the end for a pinball machine and a pay phone. Along the other side of the room were low black plastic booths with shiny black Formica-topped tables. The front one was a U-shaped job that could seat a good-sized farm family, and it well might have before the bikers took the place over. Four two-toppers filled the rest of the space between the bar and the row of booths. Dead ahead were the johns behind a tacky plywood divider covered with gold-marbled mirror tiles. I hoped I wouldn't need one. To the right was the brawl room. It was the back half of the building and it had two pool tables in the center with miscellaneous Salvation Army kitchen tables and chairs scattered haphazardly along the walls.

One table headquartered the leader of the pack and his "property." Even if his insignia hadn't been revealing, I would have known this one. He was the leader by virtue of the way he held himself. Like a shepherd with his flock, he sat there with his eyes moving around the room, unconsciously surveying his troops. About my age, I guessed, stubbly beard and almost good-looking. Probably learned to be tough in reform school and honed those skills in Nam. The property was a wispy blonde. The kind of biker chick who gravitates toward the big tough guys to shelter them under a violent male wing. She was slender, well-proportioned, and pale. Late twenties, with bluish circles under her eyes, and long, fine blond hair that was clean but hadn't seen a professional haircut in a while. If an artist had been able to widen the hazel-green eyes, halfway between what she had and Keane, and to pull her forehead and mouth into a better geometric relationship, she might have been beautiful.

He looked cunning. She looked like someone who had given up on life except to watch him to see what she should do next. He was hard but she only played at it. I guessed his IQ to be average and hers to be less than that, whether through drugs or her dependence on the leader of the pack. She was probably a great lay.

Three other tables held scruffy-looking plebes, and there were two additional couples at the bar. One guy's hand was resting on his main squeeze in an indelicate position, but she didn't seem to mind at all. The tableau would have made a great slice-of-life photograph that would make Norman Rockwell turn over in his grave.

I took a bar stool at a socially acceptable distance from the two couples. The bartender was right out of the manual. An old biker. Degenerate. Reprobate. Lots of tattoos, a healthy beard, and surly by design.

"Whaddya have?"

"Burger and a beer."

"Onions?"

"Yeah."

That was all he needed to know from me, so I was free to swivel around in the bolted-to-the-floor stool and take in the scenery. I was trying to figure out which one of these guys I could entice into walking over and saying, "Whatcha staring at, asshole?" whereupon I could start a conversation.

As it turned out, the roundheels saved me. Mimi walked out of the bathroom looking like she was in some kind of altered state, but she recognized me anyway and sauntered over. She took the stool next to mine and I looked around to see if any of the bikers were getting pissed. I invoked

49

Rule One. I didn't flirt with her, although the impulse was overwhelming. She had a lot less makeup on and a little more cleavage showing, which made for a nice combination. I let her lead.

"Hey."

"Hey, yourself."

"Didn't I see you havin' breakfast with that twerp Roscoe this morning?"

"Yup. That was me."

"What do you want with Roscoe? He sells real estate, for chrissake."

"I'm here trying to buy some real estate."

"Honey, people who have enough bread to buy real estate don't drink in this bar."

She squinted at me and I just shrugged. She decided to push it. She swiveled to face the head honcho's table.

"Hey, Arnie. This guy here says he's in Richmond to buy some real estate."

Arnie sized me up. I kept my mouth shut. We were like two dogs straining to pick up each other's scent. Finally, he growled.

"Yeah, well, tell 'im the bar ain't for sale and to get his straight ass outta here."

Mimi batted her eyelashes at me and pouted.

"Arnie says to get your straight ass outta this bar. I think you better listen to him."

Felicitously, the bartender slammed my burger on the bar, which gave me an opening gambit.

"Hey, Arnie. Okay with you if I finish my burger first?"

Arnie sighed like a beleaguered patriarch forced to deal with the rabble and walked over to my stool. The bar got real quiet, smelling the confrontation.

"I thought I told you to get outta this bar. Geek, give this guy his bill and let him take his burger with him."

Geek threw a greasy piece of paper at me and started to reach for my burger. Real helpful, old Geek.

I took my shot.

"Arnie, just let me eat this piece of dog meat here and I'll buy you all a round or two and tell you how to set that 'hard tail' out there so you can squeeze a little more high end out of it. Whatsa matter, Arnie? Doncha know how to take advantage of straight guys who are into scooters?"

Arnie backed off just a hair.

"How come you know about hard tails?"

"Saw it on the way in, used to have one myself. Only reason I stopped here was to get a better look at that bike."

"Oh, yeah? What do you ride?"

"Well, in Colorado I like to do some mountain riding, on and off the road, so I have a Husquevarna. 'Course I apologize for the rice burner with my old pan head. You want that drink or not?"

"Geek, the gentleman's buying a round. Set it up."

Arnie commandeered a third bar stool and I was in. Flanked by the pretty roundheels and big daddy, there wasn't any further danger here. He polled me about the other bikes I owned, and he drooled a little when I told him about the way I had customized the pan head. I had one more statement guaranteed to warm the cockles of any red-blooded biker's heart and cement the beginning of a friendship.

"Y'know, Arnie, the real problem is that the Japs dumped all those hunks of junk on the American road."

"Jeeeeee-zus. Tell me about it. Kawasuckies and Yamaha-has. Fuckin' tin cans, all of 'em."

We talked bikes another twenty minutes and I bought the second round. By that time, Mimi seemed to be impatient to know who I was and why I was buying real estate.

"So tell me about this gig with Roscoe, man. Why do you want to buy real estate in this hole?"

"Because I can get it cheaper here than in Kansas City.

And because I hear your Mayor looks the other way on red tape if he likes you enough."

Arnie's eyes moved ever so slightly, first left, then right. Roundheels laughed. Arnie spoke first.

"Shit, pay him enough and he'll look the other way even if he doesn't like you. I feel sorry for you, mister, if you have to spend your time dealing with assholes like McCain."

"Ah, I run a business. If you're a biker, you deal with the heat, and if you're in business, you deal with politicians. Comes with the territory."

I paused for a moment because timing is everything when you're lying.

"Say, maybe you can help me. I just met McCain, some broad from the Chamber of Commerce, and the top cop. I start to fall asleep when people like that go into their dog and pony show. I need to know who really runs this town and what really goes on here. Straight shit—not some public-relations crap. Y'know what I mean?"

Mimi looked at me with considerable intelligence in her eyes, mascara and all.

"What kind of business are you in?" she asked.

"Manufacturing."

"Manufacturing what?"

"Precision machine parts that go into rockets and missiles aimed at the Soviet Union. Among other things."

She frowned but Arnie pounded me on the back and gave me an "Attaboy!" Biker patriotism is one of the weirdest phenomena I've ever encountered, but it's there like a silent vigilante force. If the Russkies ever marched on Missouri, the bikers would be on the front line with chains, tire irons, and Saturday night specials. Not to mention more sophisticated weaponry that's made its way into the subculture via the disaffected Nam vets that the "one-percenters" have attracted since the war.

"So what's that got to do with who runs Richmond?" Mimi asked.

"There's a fine line between organized street crime and organized white-collar crime," I told her. "I need to put this plant somewhere that's safe from those Italian boys whose capo fathers put them through Harvard Business School and now let them run the cleaner side of the business."

She was nodding as if she knew something about that, and Arnie was suddenly staring off into space.

"I'm looking at four towns and so far all of them are too close to big cities. This one is probably too damned close to Kansas City, but forty miles fits better with my definition than the others. It might work. Anyway, when I go into a town, I find out who runs drugs, who's sleeping with who, and which cops are on the take from whom. Then I know where I stand with the white-collar spies who usually come out of other divisions of the same organizations."

I paused again because Arnie had his lips pursed in a strange sour-lemon way. I decided to ask for some empathy.

"So anyway, that's why I need to know all that shit, and I'll understand if you don't really give a damn and don't want to talk about that stuff."

He remained silent. She looked uncomfortable. It was no time to push it. A couple of drinks and a discussion of motorcycles makes for only the most fragile of alliances. I ran my hand over my face and rubbed my eyelids, then looked straight at Arnie and decided to play a trump.

"If you can't give me information, I'd surely appreciate you pointing me to a couple of white crosses. I been on the road too long."

Now, there was no particular reason why a biker should give me a controlled substance when I'd just told him that I'd been speaking with the Chief of Police that afternoon.

Hell, I was as strange a stranger as they'd seen in some time. On the other hand, you don't get to be Big Daddy without having some sense about who's a narc, who's setting you up, and who's a real amoral outlaw. And I've never seen a biker without a lead on whites—fact is, they seem to control most of it in this country.

Arnie motioned to his property, who sidled up on cue. He reached into her bra, retrieved a cloth pouch, reached into it with the first two fingers of his big paw, and handed me a small folded paper. She stood stock still, like a passive vessel who lived to contain things that other people wanted to store in or on her body.

"Try this. It's a helluva lot better."

"Thanks."

The built-in safety valve for Arnie in the whole transaction was that he still had time on his own turf to see whether I'd wash down the powder with what remained of my beer. If I didn't do it on the spot, I'd be in a world of hurt. If I did, I'd be one wired dude. It was worth it. Arnie knew stuff. I needed to have him trust me. I managed to poke some of it into my cheek, but the rest went down the hatch.

"Arnie, my man, you saved the day. Hate to leave your charming company, but I've got lots to do tonight and more tomorrow. I hate to waste good drugs that way, but thanks for the pop."

I took a shot at the bartender, who was probably the grand old man of this crew.

"Yo, Geek."

"Yeah?"

"I think I saw another scroungy German shepherd down the street that you can use for tomorrow's burgers."

That was worth a guffaw from the audience, an eye twinkle from Arnie, and a friendly bird from Geek.

I got off my stool. Mimi put her hand on my arm.

"Is Roscoe trying to sell you any of Casey's land?"

"Yep. So far it's the best thing he's shown me."

She cocked her head.

"Just be careful, stranger."

"I'm always careful."

Arnie stood up.

"What's your name, bub?"

"Farber. Jim Farber."

"Well, Farber. You might want to think about putting your factory in Montana instead of Missouri. Might be easier for everybody all around. Good luck."

He lightened up suddenly like a little kid.

"You get a hold of me if you ever want to sell that pan head. Shit, I'd steal the money to buy that one."

"Deal."

I left the bar and went back to the inn, where I didn't sleep at all.

8

I met Roscoe at his downtown office, which is not to be confused with an uptown office. There were stains on the carpet, and the old upholstered armchair was losing some stuffing. I like it when a man's office reflects his character. Roscoe was unbearably cheerful.

"Howdy, Jim. You ready to kick some dirt?"

I threw some maps on his desk for effect and plopped myself down in the armchair. "Let's bag the other two pieces. It's Casey's deal or nothing. The other two parcels won't accommodate the footprint nearly as well. I don't have time to waste. I'm flying out of MCI at four this afternoon."

"Whatever you say, Jim. We'll go take a look around and

then we'll meet Casey at the home place. I'll try to set it up for eleven o'clock. We can get going right after I call unless you want some coffee."

"We'll pick it up on the way, Roscoe. Let's move."

The drive to the Casey farm was kind of pretty. As we headed out of town on Garner, I noticed a group of low brick multiplexes on the right that I had seen the day before on my tour.

"What are those, Roscoe?"

"Well, that's our gentrification project, Jim. Federally supported housing. If you ask me, all it does is screw the town out of some taxes for a few years until the property reverts to us. 'Course by then there probably won't be anything there worth revertin'."

It was pretty obvious where Roscoe stood on civil rights and equal opportunity.

We crossed a railroad track without a signal, and the road got a little less tidy and a lot more dusty. A Missouri farm bears little resemblance to a Colorado ranch. On the eastern plains of Colorado, you can see for miles. The only trees dotting the landscape are those planted under federal programs, at the behest of the county agent, to prevent topsoil wind erosion. Missouri's rolling hills are covered with mature trees. Fields are furrowed between the woods once they have been carved out of the lush foliage.

The Casey place was not exactly what I had expected. It was set off by a huge white-pillared house with green shutters that looked like a movie set for *Gone With the Wind*. It was on a knoll way back from the road. Roscoe had presented the ground fairly. It was lightly rolling, and a fair amount had been cleared for farming. Cattle roamed on some of it, as did some bacon. The views were pleasant and it was far enough out of town to meet my conjured-up needs for privacy and tall fences. We drove around and scoped out the neighbors. Roscoe was definitely shifting into hard sell. We got to the "home place" at ten fifty-five. The home place was half a mill worth of Tara architecture, complete with swimming pool and five-car garage. Inside was Midwestern modern, meaning that the antiques were all American and there were no fancy foreign materials like marble in the entryway.

Jack Casey opened the door himself. His Irish ancestry was written all over him. Beefy around the middle, ruddy complexioned, and hearty. If you put him in the right clothes, he could have been a beat cop in New York City during the first wave of Irish immigration. Blue eyes, charming smile. He shook my hand, nodded at Roscoe, and motioned us into the study.

"Good to meet you, Farber. When Roscoe called, I couldn't have been more surprised. Roscoe's had this ground listed so long that the listing agreement is getting yellow. Can't say I'm that anxious to sell, but what the hell. If it means jobs for Richmond, I'll talk. Have a seat. Vivian, c'mere!"

A young woman of about fifteen rounded the corner. She was an Irish beauty with jet black hair and creamy pale skin replete with freckles.

"Yes, Daddy?"

"Get these gentlemen whatever they want. You a drinking man, Jim?"

"Only when I'm awake, Jack."

Casey chuckled. "What's your pleasure?"

"Black Jack, if you have it."

"Two Jacks and Roscoe's usual, honey."

She looked perplexed for a moment.

"Daddy, what's Roscoe's usual?"

"It's that dusty bottle of unblended Scotch on the top shelf of the bar. There's no accounting for taste, I always say."

Roscoe apparently had dimensions I didn't know about.

This child was clearly in training to be the lady of the manor, and I suspected she was Casey's favorite.

After Vivian returned with our drinks, we settled in and began a strange negotiation. I watched Casey shift gears in a split second. One moment he was the jocular host and the next he was the tough horse trader that Roscoe had warned me about.

"You understand, Farber, that the price that Roscoe first talked to me about is ridiculously low. Now, I'm all for economic development, but I'm not about to give the land away. So unless you have some flexibility in that price, we might as well talk about football while we finish our drinks."

"Price always depends on terms, Jack. How much paper are you willing to carry?"

"None. The only way this thing makes sense is if you buy it for cash. I'm not a lender, I'm a farm implements dealer. I'm sure you understand that with recent downturns, I don't need to be carrying paper. I need to be infusing cash into my business to diversify out of this confounded agricultural crap."

"How about a two-part payout? Half at closing and half in twelve months."

"You're not listening to me, sir. I don't like to do business with people who don't listen. All cash or no sale."

Roscoe was tight-lipped, and it was now clear that he didn't control this seller any more than he controlled sunrise. There was something wrong with this picture, and I heard alarm bells going off that were real loud.

I heard Stryker-in-my-head: "When people are being irrational, throw them a bumblebee."

I stood up and grinned at Casey.

"Jack, I've got eight counties in four states courting this project like I was the best prospect they'd ever met in their lives. You've got a nice piece of ground, but it ain't the only piece of ground in this part of the world. I don't like to do business with people who don't understand the competition. I've also got a plane to catch. Roscoe? Looks like we're outta here."

Casey folded his arms and stood his ground while Roscoe dragged himself to his feet with a mournful sigh. I started out of the study toward the front door.

"Farber! Come back here, goddamn it."

I turned to face him, the very picture of indifference.

"It is not widely known, but I have partners in this particular parcel and they don't want a terms deal. Call me in a week and I'll see what I can do."

I checked Roscoe's face for the surprise that I expected to see there. I wasn't disappointed. The trusted broker didn't know anything about any partners, but he was smart enough to anchor the reprieve.

"I'll be glad to help you with that, Jack," he said. "And I'll keep Jim posted on those conversations. Thanks for the drink."

I inclined my head slightly, still cool but amicable.

"I'll expect to hear from Roscoe, then. Good-bye, Jack."

I didn't say a word until we got to the car. Then I turned on the poor schlep as any real industrial buyer would do in such a situation.

"Well, what the hell was that, Roscoe? You call that doing your homework? I have just wasted two friggin' days in a town that doesn't want to sell anything I want to buy. Why the hell didn't you tell me Casey had partners?"

"Jesus, I surely am embarrassed about all this," said Roscoe. "I didn't tell you because I didn't know. It's certainly not that way in any of the county records. I rechecked it myself yesterday while you were roamin' around town. I don't know what got into the old fart. Maybe I underestimated how much he lost in the last few years. Maybe he needs cash, but I thought he was richer than God. I can't imagine who his partners could be unless . . . "

"Unless what?"

Roscoe shrugged. "Unless it's Judge Gaiters. Jack and the Judge have been known to do a few real-estate deals now and then. But listen, Jim. You did just right back there. Just go back to Colorado and let me work on Casey. Maybe we can use this to our advantage, y'know."

I now not only had my representative by his ass pocket, I had him by his professional honor, which ain't much in commercial real estate, but it was the small advantage that I needed.

I flew back to Colorado to chat with the Foundation.

9

I looked out the window of the "Friendly Skies" Boeing 737-300 and reviewed what I had. A Mayor with bushy eyebrows and sour mash in his briefcase. A Police Chief who was treading lightly and wrote letters to the DEA. An ex–Police Chief who was in the Mayor's back pocket. A farm implements dealer with cash-flow problems. A judge who might be his invisible partner and a biker who suggested that I move the whole operation to Montana. And Mimi. My gut said that she might have more of the puzzle pieces than anyone else I'd talked to in the last two days.

My next move was to get back to Coal Creek so I could report to the fat man, so to speak. Truth is, Stryker isn't really fat. He's just stout. Size 46 portly short, and most of it dense muscle. I know. I once challenged him to let me hit him as hard as I could in the panza. The deal was that if he flinched, he bought the bourbon. I was a young and foolish man then. I ended up dislocating two knuckles, jamming a thumb, and paying off the bet.

Somewhere around Hays, Kansas, I glanced out of the window again, saw the massive alto cumulus, and I knew we were about to experience some weather. The fall snows in this part of the world can be a bitch. What I didn't know at the time was that we would circle Stapleton for an eternity before we were cleared for an ILS approach.

Denver was damn near butt deep in mashed potatoes. There were sixteen inches of snow on the ground and counting. Our captain informed us that I-70 was closed from Byers to the Kansas line because of blowing and drifting snow, and I-25 was closed north from Fort Collins to Wyoming and south over Monument Pass for the same reason, due to piss-cutter winds. The Denver Police Department was working a thirty-car accident, the five-county area was on accident alert, and the call had gone out for four-wheel-drive vehicles to volunteer to drive stranded doctors and nurses to work. And the Denver Broncos were off to another erratic season. Won in a blizzard, no snowball incidents, said it was fun in the postgame interviews. The Colorado Ski Country folks love a good early-season blizzard on national TV.

My minor amphetamine rush was long gone and I was bone weary. My four-by-four was in its own custom snowdrift in remote parking at the airport, and I wasn't looking forward to digging it out only to have that exercise followed by the long drive home in blinding, blowing snow. SH 93 across the flats is always nip and tuck in this weather. It was eight o'clock before I booted my front door open. The phone was ringing.

"This is Hopper."

"I understand it's snowing a bit there. Flurries, I think you call them."

"You bastard. Why don't you just brush the sand from between your toes, Stryker, while I try to shoulder my front door closed against the flurries that have piled up on my porch. Stand by a minute."

What I didn't tell Stryker was that sixteen inches of snow covering mountain pines and high peaks is pretty spectacular. Tomorrow night would be picture perfect. Perhaps I could find someone to share a short cross-country ski tour, a bottle of wine, and a roaring fire. I would have preferred to nurse my fantasy a bit, but Stryker was waiting for me to report. I kicked the door shut and went back to the phone.

"Okay. I didn't hook any big fish on this expedition, but I got a carp or two. I'm going back with a bigger tackle box next time."

"Can the metaphors, Hopper, and tell me what you know."

So I told him. When I got to the part about the judge, he grunted. Stryker's the only person I know who grunts meaningfully. Some grunts mean "That's nonsense" and other grunts mean "That's interesting, pursue it." I couldn't decipher this one, so I swallowed my pride and asked.

"You interested in this judge?"

"I'm interested in the gestalt. A mayor, a judge, a businessman, a good-old-boy ex-cop, and a biker. Find the D.A."

"Why the D.A.?"

"Think of what you could do with those players. Think of what could be ignored by that legal system if there were, in fact, a conspiracy. And stay in touch."

"That's it? Find the D.A. and stay in touch?"

"I see no need for superfluous conversation about the matter."

"Good to talk with you, too."

The line disconnected and I dragged myself to bed and dreamt of enigmatic redheads and riding Arnie's hard-tail Harley down the canyon.

10

The next morning the sky was blue, the sun was shining, and by ten o'clock the temperature had climbed to twenty-seven degrees. The airport had a runway or two open and was trying to unload a terminal that looked like a rescue mission on a bad Saturday night. It's times like these that make you glad you're not a ticket agent.

I set about preparing for a longer stay in Richmond. The old inn in Excelsior would do as home base. I needed tools and a few more comforts from home. Weaponry always stirs up a debate. Guns are crude, not nearly as elegant as the dance of a ninja or small sharp instruments. I took one anyway, a .25 Colt automatic with hand-loaded cross-hatched hollow points, complete with boot and wallet holsters. Next I selected a few other toys, including lock picks, regular and IR scopes, a spring-driven stiletto that looked like a ballpoint pen, plus a few miscellaneous tools. I also packed my "born to be wild" clothes—the well-worn black T with the Harley symbol and a bottle of Black Jack screened onto the chest, and my older leather jacket with the requisite number of zippers and buckles. Somehow I didn't feel that the elkskin Hein Gericke with the zippered vents would fit in too well with Arnie's crowd. With any luck, I might get a turn on Arnie's machine.

I had some phone calls to make. It was time to stop screwing around with second-hand information. I needed to have a conversation with the mysterious intermediary. I stopped throwing things into suitcases and dialed up Lawless in D.C. I may not worship Mike the way he would like me to, but I sure like the way he wears his style.

"Lawless office."

I always smirk when I hear Cherise answer his phone that way. Law-less office, indeed.

Cherise was one of those Washington women who garnered all her self-esteem by working for a powerful man. They work with the dedication of a good hunting dog and seldom marry. She always seemed a little smarter than that, but I didn't know her well. If I'd ever had a spare weekend in D.C., I would have spent it on Cherise.

"Cherise, this is Hopper. Is the man in?"

"No, Hopper. He's with the Mexican consul."

"What's he doing with the Mexican consul, my dear?"

"Taking a steam."

"Have him call me, please."

"Certainly. May I tell him which number to use?"

"I'm in Colorado."

"In Cold Creek?"

"No, dear, that's *Coal* Creek."

"Hey, I was born in Newark. Gimme a break."

"Only if you tell Mike to gimme a call."

"Will do. Bye, Hopper."

"Wait a minute, Cherise, have you ever been west of the Mississippi River?"

"I've never even been west of the Hudson River, Hopper. Is this an invitation?"

"You bet. I'm a great tour guide. I'll even show you the wonders of Coal Creek."

"Sounds like bait and switch to me. I suspect that I'd find that Coal Creek only had one wonder."

"You may be right. Maybe it's something you ought to check out for yourself. Consider it a standing invitation."

"Why do I get the feeling we wouldn't spend much time standing?"

"Because you're a perceptive woman."

She giggled.

"Good-*bye*, Mr. Hopper."

"Good-bye, Cherise. Make him call me."

I like my mountain abode, but if I ever turned into a city kid, Lawless's digs would do just fine. The brownstone was a few blocks away from the Hart Senate Building and it was designed to be his nerve center. Office on the first floor, cool and secure. Presided over by the lovely and efficient Cherise. Slick gave way to masculine elegance in the "quarters" on the second floor. The leather couches were Italian, the books were first editions, the paintings were all originals, not unlike their owner. I sighed and prepared to get back to my tasks.

There was one more potential informant that I wanted to touch base with, and I had to start with Jake Barnum to even find him. Jake has been with the Boulder County Sheriff's Department since the earth cooled. Boulder County is urban, suburban, and rural all at once, so Jake has a little more depth than the average Sheriff type.

"Boulder County Sheriff's Department."

"Chief Deputy Barnum, please."

"Under-sheriff Barnum is at a meeting at the moment. May I take a message or connect you with another deputy?"

"Holy Christ, Frieda. When did he become the Under-sheriff? And does that mean I'll never talk to him again because he'll be in some perpetual administrative meeting?"

"Well, hi there, Mr. Hopper. I didn't recognize your voice. Please hold."

She found him.

"So Jake, what's this about the ol' man promotin' you to a level at which you will be only half as effective as you were before? I don't know if congratulations or condolences are in order. I suspect you deserve it as much as anyone just for living through the previous administrations, though."

"Yeah, well, I don't like the paperwork much, but show me a man who can turn down a promotion on the county law-enforcement treadmill. It's appointed and it's political, but it's also a hell of a lot more money. Hell, my life's no worse and he gave me an interesting assignment."

"What's that, Barnum? Liaison to the League of Women Voters? I know the Peter Principle when I see it in operation."

"Just for that, Hopper, I'm probably going to deny whatever harebrained favor you have called me to ask for, comprende?"

"Now, now, Under-sheriff, sir, don't get sand in your jock. I need to find Cochise."

"Trouble?"

"Maybe."

"Local?"

"Nope."

"Well, last time I heard from him, he was in St. Louis working part-time as a rehab counselor and part-time undercover for the local strike force."

"Got a number?"

"Yeah, but you know you always have to go through three to find him. Try the Chinese restaurant at Forty-fourth and Lindburgh. It's quicker than dialing all those phone numbers and comin' up empty. They always know where he is."

"Thanks, Jake. I owe you one."

"One my ass."

I heard a click and hoped I hadn't really offended him. I could almost hear his growl as he scrunched down behind a pile of paperwork.

Cochise, a.k.a. "Little Brother," a.k.a. a lot of other names that I can't repeat, was a contact whom Jake and I developed awhile back on another matter. If he'd been in the espionage business, he would have been a triple agent. He had university degrees in psychology. We know he used. We know he dealt. We also knew he'd worked vice unofficially in at least three states and the vice guys who served as references loved him. Nobody ever quite knew where his allegiances really were. I liked him because he was an outlaw like me. Short, feisty, with premature salt-and-pepper hair. A man of many coats and hats. Drug hip.

I considered it a stroke of luck that he was in St. Louis. I wanted someone to bring me up to speed on the regional drug stuff. You can talk about the international drug- and gun-running trade and the national drug problem, but when it comes right down to it, you have to know who's moving what to whom and where. People have territories that they control just like a McDonald's franchise, and every territorial capo runs the business a little differently. A junkie is a junkie and they are infinitely adaptable, but the way the product is bought, cut, and distributed has regional styles.

If Little Brother was in St. Louis, I had a friend in court in the Midwest. Jake was right. You couldn't always find him on the phone unless you knew exactly which state agency he'd chosen to hide in. It was still worth a try. Cochise might be able to explain how designer drugs got to Richmond. After all, this is the man who owned the latest edition of the *The Drug Cookbook* by Chubaka Darth.

The phone suddenly popped off like a mouthy kid and I answered it.

"Yes."

"This is Mike Lawless."

There was something he did with the first syllable of his last name that I couldn't replicate. I'm a good mimic. It was halfway between arrogant and "Fuck you," and it marked him like a scar.

"Thanks for calling back. I need to touch your contact."

"No way."

"I thought this was a team, Lawless. Or am I just supposed to wander around poking at things with a sharp stick until something moves? It's not as if I were asking you to put this one in my lap. Quit being such a bloody jerk."

"Or perhaps you would consider not being such an impudent boor. I can't deliver him."

"Oh, horseshit!"

I was digging myself into a tactical debacle. If I had been precise and controlled in my contempt, I might have gotten somewhere with him, but for some reason he always gets under my skin. Maybe it's the way he says his name that starts it. Damned if I know, but he can always push my button pretty much at will. Maybe I was just frustrated and suspicious.

Lawless can deliver anyone. I wouldn't even put Jimmy Hoffa or Stalin's ghost beyond his reach. I've never understood why he needs to structure every interaction like it's a war, but that's what he does. He continued.

"Sorry you feel that way, Hopper, but that's the way it is."

"So give me more background. So far all I know is that there's this town in Missouri that doesn't seem right to you. All that surfaces is the penny-ante stuff that small municipalities are made of. Nickel-and-dime corruption at best. I got a letter from a police chief to the DEA. I got a bureaucratic response. I got a picture of the town whore. I got a photo of a federal agent who got in the way of a little bomb that made him into something only a pit bull could love. Stryker wants me to call on the D.A. Hell, I got nothin', Lawless. The only thing I've counted on is that Stryker says you have a credible source who thinks Richmond might be a factory town on the Kansas City pipeline. If it's any less than that, I don't know why I'm wasting my time on this one."

My voice got a little louder, but now I was doing it on purpose. Lawless was going to give or Professor Stephens was going to have some explaining to do. And then Lawless did something I hate.

"Have you discussed this with Stryker?"

"No, and I haven't discussed it with the Pope either, Michael. So far I don't have any reason to spend Foundation money on this mission, and I'm not going to do it because the Bobbsey Twins think it's a good idea. Got it?"

There was a pregnant pause and I could see, in my mind's eye, Mike Lawless factoring the possibilities. I just let him factor, content to be silent and ominous on my end.

"Hopper, you are always difficult."

"Yes, and it always seemed to suit my colleagues."

"Except for me."

"Yeah, except for you. Do I get your contact or not?"

"He'll be in touch."

"*Muchisimas gracias por nada, embajador.*"

"Hmph."

It took all my willpower not to call Cabo. I finished packing and sat tight.

11

The one thing I've never been able to master in my life is sitting on my hands. I've done it when I've had to and I can control the critical systems like breathing and heart rate. It takes a hell of a lot of concentration and internal energy. I was now trapped in Lawless's time line and I didn't like it one bit. I grabbed the cordless phone and a down vest, pulled on my Sorels, plowed my way to the barn, and pounded out the wrinkles in the fender of my '41 Chevy pickup until the cordless rang.

"Hello?"

"Is this Hopper?"

"Depends on who's calling."

"Lawless asked me to get in touch with you."

The voice was deep and confident. It seemed very familiar, but it didn't evoke a name or a face for me. I probed.

"Have we met?"

"Not to my knowledge."

"And just what part of the political world do you live in?"

"Sorry, not relevant."

"Look, I'm trying to be of some assistance to your DEA guy. Don't you think a little cooperation might be in order?"

"I'll tell you anything I know, but if I wanted to be identified, I would have invited you to breakfast."

"Fair enough, but I could do without all this Deep Throat stuff."

He laughed. I suspected he was an attorney from Justice. One of the older ones who came up with Lawless in the sixties. I couldn't prove it, and in some ways he was right: It didn't matter.

"Start with whatever makes you think the Police Chief isn't trying to feather his own nest," I said, "and tell me why the DEA guy bothered to contact you if the Agency wasn't interested in pursuing this matter."

"The second part is easier than the first. Ron Gable has been an agent for ten years, but he comes from a big-city vice background, which means he gets impatient with the decision-makers in the Eye St. Building. He's not known as a hothead or a crazy, so sometimes they listen to him. Often they don't. They wouldn't buy off on the Richmond investigation for a variety of reasons, which Ron tells me is a product of their internal politics. So he called me. I've gotten a couple of things done for him before because I think he's the kind of guy whose instincts are still pretty sharp."

"How does he know Doug Ketchum?"

"Apparently, they cooperated on an interjurisdictional

sting operation that netted quite a few drug entrepreneurs in North Kansas City. The collar was so clean that the DEA had very little trouble wiring a couple of kingpins who they've been onto forever. I guess Ron figured he owed Doug one."

"What do you make of the letter that Ketchum sent Gable? It didn't say much. And why write a letter? Why not just pay Gable a visit?"

"Ketchum did pay Gable a visit. Ron asked for the letter to have something to show his superiors. Ketchum typed it himself—"

"Yeah, you can tell."

"—and delivered it personally."

"So the critical question is what else did Ketchum tell Gable in person that persuaded Ron to go to further trouble to help him?"

"Simply that there were massive amounts of dope being processed somewhere in the vicinity of Richmond on their way to Kansas City and the rest of the network, and that he couldn't proceed with his own investigation because he thought some Richmond bigshots were involved, including the one who signed his check."

"How involved? Looking-the-other-way involved or getting-their-hands-dirty involved?"

"Hands on and real dirty."

"How does the dead agent fit in?"

"The K.C. district agent was killed two days after Doug saw him coming out of a biker bar just outside of Richmond. Maybe there's a connection, and maybe the guy just went in to have a beer."

"How did Doug make the DEA guy at the bar? They knew each other?"

"Enough to nod to. The dead agent was an ancillary part of the sting operation. That's all I know."

"All right. That's more helpful than you realize, and I

appreciate it. Just off-the-record, why did you call Mike? I'm sure you have other contacts."

He paused. I was either okay or I wasn't.

"I served under Lawless in Navy intelligence—and don't try to look it up, because our work is still so classified it never existed."

I played a hunch.

"And if I mentioned the name Stryker Stephens?"

He chuckled. "I'd accuse you of name-dropping. Best of luck."

The line went dead and I finally noticed that I was still in the barn freezing my ass off. I went in to finish packing. By the time I headed for the airport, the plow had been through, but the four-wheel-lock still felt good underfoot. I wonder when Coal Creek Canyon will get scheduled limo service. Hah.

12

I declined the offered airline "snack" and sipped slowly on a double Jack rocks. I had some decisions to make. The next few moves would color the rest of the operation. I had to have an ally now who could be persuaded to help with details. Roscoe was fine as a front man, but he didn't know anything.

My choices boiled down to Doug, who had the right motivation but not enough data, and Mimi, who might have the wrong motivation or no motivation at all but who probably had more information than I even wanted. I would need them both. The question was where to start.

Stryker reared his pedantic head from his private ROM somewhere in my brain. "Women are better at quickly seeing the whole picture and men are better at seeing the critical detail. When you have a choice, start with a woman, end with a man."

I met my first and only wife at the Rand Corporation in Stryker's School for Spooks. When we asked to be assigned together as a counterinsurgence team, which was then against the rules, Stryker championed us, he says, for just that reason. Caitlin could size up a situation in an eye blink. And I always knew which button to push. If I'd had Caitlin, I wouldn't need Doug or Mimi, but I made it out of the Asian trenches with my lifetime supply of scars and nightmares. Caitlin didn't make it out at all. I made a mental sharp turn away from that memory and focused on my next steps.

Approaching Mimi was a touchy issue. I was convinced that she wasn't a biker's lady since bikers' ladies only trick to buy gas or food, plus no one had seemed very possessive of her at the bar. So I could go in as having fallen in lust with the lady of the night. Given my involuntary masculine reaction to the way God had put her together, I tried to remain more objective than usual about that approach since it was already my favorite. I could also work the good-time Charlie from out of town, which I rejected out of hand because I don't make a good john, even in costume and grease paint. Or I could try to be her friend, which was probably not anything she was used to in Richmond.

The landing gear went down before I'd made that decision. I was in no big hurry to let anyone know I was back in town, so I picked up the rental car and drove straight to my spring-fed home away from home and was welcomed by yet another front-desk person in training. Fortunately, there wasn't a line and the reservations were in order. I got the room I requested without having to deliver the usual dissertation on what a "civilized room" should mean in the hotel business. The Europeans know, but then they had a head start on cookbook-formula graduate-school hotelry.

Ah, Mimi...I'd had great luck just running into the woman wherever I went, but now I was going to have to look for her. I couldn't call Roscoe because that would tip him off to my presence, and I couldn't call information because I didn't know her last name.

Then I remembered Geek. But it was dark and late, and at the moment his bar was probably full of the black-leather, dirty-jean, scruffy-boot, trucker-wallet, chain-and-zipper gang, which wouldn't suit my purposes, so instead I arranged my portable office, put an outline for tomorrow on paper, and got some sleep.

The next morning I flipped through the Yellow Pages and found a couple of bars that could be in the right neighborhood, one under "Taverns" and one under "Lounges." I guess AT&T still can't bring itself to call a friggin' bar a bar in the Bible Belt. It was the one listed under "Lounges" that I decided on. It was the most ludicrous. I realized that Geek had a sense of humor after all. He'd named the bar The Leather Lounge. Mind you, there's no sign on the building that says LEATHER LOUNGE, only a rusted tin arrow framing an inset with small burlesque lights outlining the arrow and spelling out BAR over faded, peeling, red block letters. I dialed the number as I selected my shirt for the day. It was about nine-thirty. The voice that answered sounded asleep.

"Yeah."

"Zis Geek?"

"Yo."

"What time do you open, Geek? Just got into town and I could use a drink."

"Who the mutha—"

"Doesn't matter, man, just tell me when you open and I won't bother you till then."

"Eleven, shithead. You better spend a lot." He slammed the phone down. I suspected he wasn't a member of Shelley's Chamber of Commerce, being outside the city limits and outside almost everybody else's limits as well.

I was not looking forward to ninety minutes of nothing, so I used all the tricks I use when I'm out of town and waiting for something to happen. I did a little t'ai chi. I shaved with my Italian designer razor. I dressed and went down to the lobby to get a cup of coffee and read the *Richmond Daily News*. I could have learned more by reading a four-year-old *Enquirer*. Time eventually passed.

I didn't leave until eleven. I figured I'd give the guy a few extra minutes to scratch his balls and finish a cold draw or two before he opened.

I walked in and I was the only customer. Not only was I the only customer, but Geek was nowhere to be seen. I sat on a stool and swiveled it so it squeaked. I started to whistle so I wouldn't startle him when he walked in.

Just as I was gettin' to the "Jeremiah was a bullfrog and a good friend of mine" part, the hulk stood up from behind the bar, where he was probably looking for his rose-colored contact lenses.

He looked through me as if I wasn't really there.

"So Geek, gimme a beer. It was a long, dry trip from L.A. Shitty service on the red-eye. I think the stews all sleep on those. I'll take a Stroh's if you got it."

He still didn't speak, but he grabbed a Stroh's from the dilapidated cooler and set it in front of me. Stroh's is brewed in Detroit. I have a friend from Detroit who says that they ought to pour it back in the horse, but bikers seem to be partial to it.

He slammed a few things around in back of the bar and finally deigned to acknowledge me.

"Thought you was from Colorado."

Ah, he remembered me after all.

"I am from Colorado. Doesn't stop me from doin' business elsewhere. Have you seen Mimi?"

"Which one?"

"The redhead with the good body."

"Sure. Seen her last night. Whatcha want with Mimi?"

He stopped and glared at me, and for a moment I thought maybe I had it wrong about her not being a biker's old lady.

"Hey, man. I don't want to get outta line here. If she's shacked up with Arnie..."

He grunted. "Naw, she's not shacked up with anyone. She's just a good time. Is that what yer lookin' for?"

"Yeah, I guess. You got a phone number or something?"

Geek looked puzzled for a second and then dug out a glass with a bunch of little scraps of paper in it. He shuffled through it and threw one next to my beer glass. It said "Mimi C." It had only four numbers after it. I looked at Geek.

"So where's the rest of the number?"

"Don't need no more'n at. Only one exchange here."

I memorized it, gave him back the paper, and finished my beer in silence.

I dropped three bucks on the bar and started to leave.

"If you don't find her at home, she's usually here most nights."

Like I said, real helpful, old Geek.

13

Geek was right: The town of Richmond had only one telephone exchange. I found that out when I checked the phone book. The rest of my search required a very boring minute and a half during which I read through the "C's" and found an M. Curtis with a phone number that matched the one Geek kept in his glass.

I checked my map and found that she lived off the main drag through town. I dialed the number from a pay phone.

"Hello?"

Her voice sounded tense and almost frightened. It didn't bode well for my ploy of being the swain.

"Hi, Mimi. This is Jim Farber. Did I call at a bad time?"

"Who?"

"Jim Farber. You remember the guy who's stupid enough to buy real estate in Richmond?"

"Oh, yeah. I remember. Listen, this has been a pretty crazy morning. I'm—uh—well, what was it you wanted?"

She sounded distracted and distressed but not under the influence of anything.

"Well, I was in town and I just thought I might buy you dinner or lunch or something."

"That's very nice of you, but you see I'm . . . I'm . . . "

Just then something snapped and she started to sob. I listened to the quality of her crying. It was semi-hysterical and very mournful. I cursed my training, which did not allow me any sympathy, just a focused attempt to figure out how I could use it. She was still crying. I had to act quickly.

I reached for a hypnotic technique that would position her where I wanted her. Most people think hypnosis requires swinging sparkling crystal balls or Grandad's old pocket watch and smoothly murmuring some hocus-pocus. Those of us who practice it know that it is simply a matter of bypassing the ego and speaking directly to the unconscious.

"Listen to me, Mimi." I said it in my very best baritone. The decibel level dropped although she was still sniveling. "You don't know me very well, but you're upset and I can help you. I'm going to be at your house in ten minutes and I don't want you to leave. I want you to stay there until I arrive, and then if you don't want to let me in, that's okay. Just stay where you are, do you understand?"

"Y–y–yes." She breathed once very deeply and I could almost see her struggle for self-control over the phone line.

"Easy, baby, stay easy. I'll be there soon."

I cradled the phone, grabbed the map, and ignored the speed limit. Richmond was getting crazy on me already.

I wasn't sure I liked it, but it beat sitting around waiting for something to happen.

I turned off of East Main at Tribble and swung left at a gravel road just behind Dear Grade School. Her house was an unimaginative little postwar frame job with four pillars and a railed porch across the front. There was a small windowed dormer centered over the front door. It was a crisp white. The address was 116 Trigg. As I walked to the door, I was aware that I was beginning to allow my curiosity to shift to concern for what had caused her tears.

When Mimi answered the door, there wasn't any question. There was a welt on the side of her neck and her left eye was black and blue. It was all the more noticeable because redheads have that delicate skin that shows every broken capillary.

In the short time it had taken me to get there, she had composed herself, and now I was looking at the Ice Woman, who was dry-eyed. She let me in with some disdain.

I elected to say nothing because any chatter at this point would just harden her resolve to be cool and in control when I needed her to tell me things that only come out when someone is scared or angry. I didn't even know what those things were, but I was even more firmly convinced than before that she knew them.

"So, Farber. I'm sorry about the phone call. It's a bad day, y'know. Just a bad goddamned day. Ya wanna cup of coffee or something?"

"I'd rather know who did this to you."

"Why? What are you gonna do, Galahad? Tackle him?"

"Maybe I will. I don't much like guys who beat on women."

She winced then and I looked away to scan the environment. What I saw pulled me up short. Nothing sat right with what I knew about her so far. It was neither the house of a hooker nor a roundheels. Conservative and well-ordered, it had bookcases with books that no habitué of biker bars should have. She caught me looking and it seemed to startle her.

"So what about that coffee? Or maybe you just wanna leave and come back some other day."

"Coffee's fine," I said. "I suspect that you would rather not parade that around town during lunch hour, huh?"

"You're right. There's no food in this town worth eating, and besides, I'm not a fan of sitting in restaurants with my sunglasses on. Thanks anyway. How come you're back in Richmond? I hear Casey doesn't want to sell."

"Who'd you hear that from?"

"Luther Brock."

"Why would Luther Brock know anything about it?"

"Luther knows a little bit about everything."

"And why did you happen to be talking to Luther?"

"Oh, no particular reason. He just sent the arresting officer this time."

"Arresting officer?"

She turned to me in mock disgust. Underneath it, I saw a woman who was right on the edge.

"Come off it, Farber. You're here because you want to get boffed. You're here because Roscoe Morton has a big mouth and then you saw me in the bar with all those animals and you made a few assumptions. Well, have at it, bud. It's fifty a roll and a hundred till morning. I bet you've paid a lot more and I bet you've paid a lot less. And I bet that's cut-rate where you come from, but this is Richmond, where everything is 'reasonable.' Brock's lackey was the arresting officer on a prostitution charge, and you knew that before you asked. Now back off or go for your wallet—no cards, no credit, no out-of-state checks."

It was a great speech and I might have bought it except for her eyes, which looked like those of a terrified fawn looking down the wrong end of a Model 70 .300 Winchester Magnum.

I decided to force her to manage surprise. I walked to the kitchen and rinsed out the coffee pot and looked in various cupboards to find something that looked like a coffee can.

She followed me in.

"What are you doing?"

"Making my own coffee since you don't seem very interested in doing it yourself."

"I don't believe that I invited you to make yourself at home, Farber."

I turned on her and grabbed both shoulders.

"The name is Hopper, not Farber, and I don't manufacture anything but solutions. I think you could use a couple of solutions right about now. You want to talk about it or do you want to stand there pretending you're a longshoreman?"

Her face crumbled and her shoulders caved in and in thirty seconds I had an armful of soft female clinging to me like I was the Rock of Gibraltar. It's not a role I'm fond of, but I can do it in a pinch.

She pulled back finally and looked at me like some silly seagull whose feathers were mucked up by an oil spill.

"Who *are* you?"

"I'm a friend, Mimi. There are things going on in Richmond that have attracted the attention of a couple of my buddies. I'm here to find out what they are. If stuff's broke, I'll fix it before I go. Think of me as sort of a handyman. That's all. But I'm a friend and I think you better tell me what happened to you last night and this morning. There's a good chance that it's all related."

She looked at me in that particular way that people use when they're trying to decide whether to take a flyer and trust their intuition. She was achingly lovely, bruises and all, and I held my breath.

"Your name is ... Hopper?"

"The very same."

She grinned ruefully, disengaged herself, and finished fixing up the coffee.

"Makes you sound like a rabbit."

"Don't be fooled. I'm really a rare cross between a leopard, a snake, and your imagination."

"I'll bet you are."

She poured two cups of decent Vienna roast and we sat at the kitchen table.

"So tell me what happened," I said.

"Nothing unusual. Brock has a couple of Doug's guys who are still in his pocket, so they pick me up and deliver me to the judge at night court and I get out if I put out. This time the judge got real nasty because I wasn't willing to ... Ah, it doesn't matter. You see, sometimes Brock's guys pick me up when I'm with a john and sometimes they pick me up just because the judge wants me that night. Tell me again why you're interested in this."

"Why don't you go public with it?"

"And what do you think the word of Mimi Curtis, nefarious party girl, would be worth in this town up against the honorable Judge Gaiters?"

"So why don't you just do the time?"

"Because if they got motivated, they could arrange some real hard time on a habitual-offender basis. It's not worth it. Mostly what I do for him is no worse than ... "

"What you do for anybody else?"

She stared away.

"Thought about moving? Thought about a straight job?"

"Yeah, I've thought about it. Then I stop thinking about it."

She pulled her hair back behind her ears and I could see remnants of a willful child.

It occurred to me that she could have plied her trade in St. Louis or K.C. for a lot more money without the same hassles. Whatever was keeping her in Richmond was not something I was likely to learn in the first half hour.

"So, Hopper, what's your number? What things are happening in Richmond that don't happen everywhere else? Are you FBI, DEA, CIA, or just an SOB?"

"No, I'm a crusader for truth, justice, and the American way. Although I have to admit that I preferred my mother's icebox strawberry pie to apple."

"Look, you're making me nervous about what I just told you. If you're a cop, play fair and tell me that."

She had a point, and I wouldn't get any more if I didn't make it right.

"Mimi, I'm here because somebody in Richmond thinks that the folks who run this town are using this cute little out-of-the-way paradise to make a ton of money doing stuff that would attract attention and land them in Leavenworth if they did it elsewhere."

"So that's why you were pumping me and Arnie at the bar?"

"Yes. Sorry about the cloak-and-dagger bit, but I had to decide who to trust. You're it, if you're interested."

"Why should I be interested?"

I shrugged and got up from the table to make my way back to the bookshelves in the living room. She followed with her coffee cup. I semi-randomly plucked a copy of *Remembrance of Things Past* from the middle shelf and leafed through it.

"So how come a small-town roundheels knows words like 'nefarious' and reads Proust?" I continued surveying her bookshelves without looking at her. "Let's see, there's also Freud, Alvin Toffler, Barbara Tuchman, and John D. McDonald. I would have thought Harlequin romances would have been more up your alley. But of course there's no law against—"

"Stop it!"

I turned to look at her.

"Where'd you go to school, Mimi?"

"Columbia, not that it's any of your business."

"Graduate?"

"Magna cum laude, for all the good it did me."

"Degree?"

"Master's in early-childhood education, minor sociology. Make your point, Hopper. I'm tired of you making judgments about things you know nothing about."

Stryker calls it "mobilizing personal history." If you can pull up a bit of personal history that has long been denied, you can use it to motivate people. Doesn't matter whether the history is honorable or sleazy. To be effective, it just has to be denied. In Mimi's case, it was an honorable piece of personal history. She had an intellect that she didn't use much anymore, and I was going to get her to use it. First, I was going to play to her wish to be helpful. All women have it. Then I was going to give her something interesting to think about.

"Look, Mimi, I'm in a spot. I can get this job done all by my lonesome, but it's going to cost me a lot of time. If you decide to help me, I can get it behind me before the week is out. I just want to know everything you know about McCain, Gaiters, Brock, and anyone else with any clout."

"You forgot two."

"Who's that?"

"Casey and Lavelle."

"I know Casey. Who's Lavelle?"

"The D.A."

Damn Stryker anyway.

14

We poured more coffee and settled into the antique armchairs in the living room.

"Tell me what you're looking for, Hopper, and we'll see if I know anything about it. I'm not going to give you everyone's life history if it isn't relevant."

"Do you like any of those people?"

"No."

"So what's to protect?"

"That depends on what you're looking for. Drugs or other vices?"

"Well, they generally go together, but for the time being, I'm looking for a high-end drug operation with a fancy facade."

"Like I said, what do you want to know about who?"

It occurred to me that if we were going to discuss drugs in Richmond, Arnie's name might come up and he was someone she might very well want to protect. I decided to take a direct shot.

"Look, Mimi, if you're worried about Arnie, we can make a deal that might work for both of us."

"Who said I was worried about Arnie?"

"I did."

"Okay, what's the agreement?"

"If Arnie and the boys are just into biker mode and dealing some for their friends and relatives, I won't touch them. If I find out that they're heavily involved in something larger, you don't hold me to it."

She tilted her head as if she thought better with it cocked.

"That's fair enough."

We talked for about an hour and I got an earful of small-town politics. Casey put McCain into office using the country-club crowd. Ketchum's appointment to Chief of Police had been an attempt to spare Brock a trial in the press because of some "misuses" of police department funds. Gaiters was an old crony of McCain's, but his appointment to the bench pre-dated the Mayor. Lavelle was married to Casey's wife's youngest sister. They had all been born and raised in the county, and had left only for brief vacations to get education or to help Uncle.

We reviewed all the rumors she knew. That Brock took bribes and still controlled about half of Ketchum's police force. That Lavelle ignored evidence if your last name was right. That McCain had a weakness for fast cars that he shouldn't have been able to afford on his combined income from apparent sources. It was all penny ante except for the judge demanding sexual favors from the girls he threw in the slammer. It was contemptible, but it was still penny ante.

"We still haven't talked about Arnie," I said. "Maybe you'd better tell me what you know I'll find."

"If you pull his record, you'll find all that stuff you call being in 'biker mode.' He deals to his friends. The only difference is . . . "

I just waited. She was getting to the hard part apparently.

"The only difference is that the cops used to harass Arnie and the other guys who run with him all the time. They'd write chickenshit tickets for loitering, littering, and spitting on the street. Just any crappy thing they thought they could get away with that would increase the hassle factor. Lavelle would make a case and Gaiters would lock one of them up to teach the others a lesson. Then it just stopped."

"How long ago?"

"About two years. Maybe two and a half."

"Why?"

"I don't know, but it seemed weird."

For a moment she seemed hard again, unwilling to risk any information that might get her or her friends into a tight spot.

"Did you ask Arnie?"

"Yeah, once, in a roundabout way. He just fed me all that biker crap about how if you lived outside the system, then the system couldn't get to you."

"What do you make of it?"

"I think Arnie cut some kind of deal."

She looked a little sad then, as if bikers cutting deals with the establishment meant that there were no longer any real outlaws, and therefore no point to her own rebellion.

I rose and she jumped up from her chair as if she wanted to beat me to the door.

"I'll call you tonight. I want to make a phone call, pay a little visit to Doug Ketchum, and then let Roscoe do some more bird-dogging for me. Are you okay?"

"Hell, if I'm not, I'll fake it. If you don't reach me, I'll be at Geek's maybe. I'm going to take the night off, if you know what I mean."

I leaned over and kissed her nose for absolutely no other reason than that it was there.

"Hey."

"Hey, yourself."

"You still haven't told me who you work for."

"And I probably never will. Is that a problem?"

She grinned. "Not unless you're working for the wrong side."

"There is no wrong side, Mimi, just sides. Lots and lots of sides."

15

I dug through the stuff I had neatly filed in the trunk of the T-bird to retrieve a home phone number for Doug that had been included in the packet Sergio had given me. I'd started with the woman and her global perceptions. Now it was time to talk to the man.

After a few rings, a woman answered.

"Is Chief Ketchum in?" I asked her.

"Sure is. May I tell him who's callin'?"

"This is Jim Farber from Colorado."

There was a bit of a wait. I hoped that Doug wasn't doing something recreational to relieve the tension of his job. I felt bad about disturbing him, because a police chief doesn't often get much of that kind of relief.

"Howdy, Jim. What can I do for you?"

"I'm actually hoping to do something for you. Can you meet me in an hour at the Elms? You might want more than a cup after this one. I'm sorry to be cutting into your time off. I'll be in the upstairs bar unless you want to go downstairs to hide."

He paused. "Okay, I'll be there. We can start upstairs."

"Apologize to your missus for the fact that I'm luring you away from the hearth. I just don't think this is normal-business-hours stuff. The walls have ears and all that."

"No problem, Jim. She's been a cop's wife for a long time. See you in an hour."

I spent the time I had in the steam room. Some of Richmond squeezed itself out of my pores. Recruiting Doug Ketchum would be a challenging tightrope walk. I had to get him to trust me when there was no reason for him to do it. I had to blast through the small-town reserve and the law-enforcement ethic. I didn't have much leverage except for the almost-truth. I got to the Elms about ten minutes early and settled myself at a small table just past the massive wooden bar. It was quiet and out of the way.

Doug walked in a few minutes later, but it took him a while to get to the table because the regulars and barmaids all had something to say to him. He was wearing jeans and a plaid shirt and they were as crisp and pressed as his city uniform. He lowered himself into the chair across the table from me.

"Howdy."

"Glad you could come."

The waitress sidled up. I ordered another Jack. Doug ordered a Scotch. He waited until the drinks had been delivered.

"So what you got, Jim?"

He looked at me like a predator staring at a victim. It was time to deal.

"Ever hear of Ron Gable?"

I gotta hand it to him. He was a Cool Hand Luke. The look on his face gave me nothing. He was so good at "no response," he might have been my cousin. Would have done Stryker's heart good to watch it. He stared at me for a while before he finally spoke.

"Yeah, maybe. Ron Gable works for the DEA. What's that got to do with a manufacturer lookin' to buy some real estate?"

"I'm not."

He looked down at his drink, his eyes wrinkled at the corners like a ten-year-old wallet, and he laughed.

"Yeah. I figured. So who the hell are you, asshole?"

"I'm trying to help Gable help you. Not through the usual channels."

"That and fifty cents'll buy you a cup a coffee."

"I understand. Would it help you any to know that I've read your letter to Gable?"

Ketchum shrugged. "What letter is that?"

The only skill that Stryker ever taught me that I can now do better than he is instant photographic recall. It makes the master nuts. I recited Ketchum's letter to him verbatim. He wavered, but he still wasn't buying.

"That's a nice script. So now I know you're a member of the Screen Actors Guild. Maybe Ron Gable ain't the man I think he is or maybe you paid off some assistant at DEA to get it. So what?"

He wasn't hostile. He looked more like a guy who wanted to believe me but needed a better reason.

"Fair enough. If you want to check me out, call this number. Ask for Under-sheriff Barnum in Boulder County, Colorado. Ask him about B. F. Hopper. Call collect person to person and say you're me. If he's there, he'll take the call."

Doug looked skeptical, but he strolled behind the bar

and commandeered the telephone. He turned his back away from the bartender. I watched him pivot and mutter into the mouthpiece. He was no more than a minute, which meant he asked questions fast. He made one more phone call and I could see from the movement of his fingers that it was long-distance information. He was making sure that the number I had given him was really the Boulder County Sheriff's Department and that I hadn't set it up beforehand.

He walked back to the table and sat down. He took a pull at his drink, tapped a cigarette out of the pack, lit up, and took a long drag.

"Barnum said if you had a small scar underneath your left ear, you were the real thing. I noticed the scar right off. He also said to watch you closely because you were a notorious sidewinder. Talk to me, Hopper. I'm runnin' outta time."

His eyes were burning holes in my game plan. He was going to trust me some now but not without more story.

"I don't think it will take long, Doug. Gable really did contact a guy in Washington who contacted another guy who contacted me."

"Who do you work for? Barnum said you're not his."

"I don't work for anyone you know."

"Look, maybe this soldier of fortune routine works in Colorado, but it don't work here. Barnum says you're not a bad guy, but that doesn't make you a good guy."

I decided to take another tack.

"You know Mimi Curtis?"

He laughed. "Jesus Christ, you've only been in town a few days and you already found Mimi. What a piece a work that one is."

"Are you aware that Brock uses some of your boys to pick her up and deliver her to Gaiters so he can get his honorable rocks off?"

His smile disappeared. He looked at me hard and then looked away. He knew damned well what was going on and it stuck in his throat. For a decent chief of police not to have enough control of his force to protect the town whore from the town's judge is unthinkable for a lawman. I had him one down and he knew it. Now that I'd put that hook in his mouth, I had to reel him in.

"So, Ketchum, I think that makes you a good guy in a tight spot. I think the same about me. If we can get past the soldier of fortune crap, we might be able to do something worthwhile."

He took a sharp breath and I knew I had him.

"Jesus, she pisses me off. She's not a dumb broad, y'know. She could do something else if she wanted. I tried to talk her into leaving town, making a new start. She wasn't having any of it. What a waste."

"How come she hangs out with Arnie?"

Doug snorted. "Y'ever take a good look at them side by side?"

I pulled up the mind's-eye image of Mimi and put it next to an image of Arnie. Superficially there wasn't much. Different hair color, different bone structure, different build. But you could see it in the eyes. I whistled softly through my teeth the way my old man taught me.

"Same daddy, Doug?"

"Nope. Same mama. I got to admit that Mimi comes by her trade rather naturally. Had the perfect role model. Her mama used to work out of a trailer over by Orrick. God knows what those kids saw. But they never went hungry."

He shook his head and I understood that Mimi's loyalty was not to a biker chieftain but to her younger half-brother.

"So tell me why you went to Gable in the first place," I said.

"It wasn't any one thing. Used to be that we had drugs

like any other small town. We had a few housewives who
got off on Valium and a few kids who liked to drink beer
and smoke a joint or two. But a couple of years ago, things
began to change. It wasn't long after I was in the job that
we began to get some real trash moving into town. We'd
do a bust and they'd have all kinds of shit that didn't
belong here, the kind of thing you'd have to go to K.C. or
St. Louie to get. I stay pretty tight with the county guys
and they were seeing the same thing. It didn't make sense.
The junkies were moving to Richmond because they could
score easier. But there weren't enough of them to make
this a big enough market for K.C. to pay attention to, so
I figured that there was a lab here and the trash knew it."

"So what's that got to do with City Hall?"

Doug grunted his disgust. "By the time we ran off most
of the trash, all the new designer shit was in the schools
anyway. We did a real clean collar on a nineteen-year-old
who was caught selling Ecstasy to a high-school kid. The
parents brought the kid in and he confessed to buying the
drugs and named the dealer. The next thing I knew, Lavelle, the D.A., was throwing the case out. Not enough
evidence, he said. Well, a week later the kid recanted, the
nineteen-year-old left town, and we were all done. It's happened a few times more since then."

"What'd you do?"

"I went to McCain first and he just blew me off. Bad for
the town, he said. Then I went to Gaiters and I had to
listen to a lecture on how I was badmouthing a fine public
servant. Lavelle and I were hardly speaking."

"Anything else?"

"Yeah, Luther Brock got drunk and assaulted a white
boy in a bar with a knife because Luther claimed the kid
was a faggot. Nice kid. Known him all my life. Christ, I
couldn't even get Brock arraigned. I nearly quit over that
one, but my wife talked me out of it."

"Was there a last straw before you went to Gable?"

"Yeah. I was pissed off when the DEA guy bit the big one on my turf when nobody bothered to tell me he was in town."

"I hear you. Seems to me, though, that this is a pretty small town to hide a lab in. Why didn't you just go after it?"

"Well, under the circumstances I wasn't going to be getting any warrants from Gaiters and . . . well, shit, half my guys still belong to Brock. The ones who belong to me did as much of an informal search as we could do without getting the wind up at Lavelle's office. It ain't easy."

His face was weary. We sat in silence for a while and then the waitress came back looking as though she was pleased to be bearing an important message.

"You're wanted on the phone, Chief."

Doug walked back to the bar. He took the call, and when he came back, he was wearing a look that I recognized.

"I gotta roll, Hopper. Sorry."

"What's up? Judging from your face, I'd say it was at least a homicide."

He looked startled and then he looked a little embarrassed. No good cop who's into "serve and protect" likes to admit it, but there is nothing more uniquely intriguing than a dead body and no suspect. It's the stuff law-enforcement war stories are made of.

I saw a moment's hesitation on his face and then it cleared.

"You wanna ride with me, Hopper?"

"I'm supposed to be a real-estate guy, remember? Wouldn't look real good to show up with the Chief on a professional call. Who died?"

"Arnie's property. Name of Slew. Facedown in a field. Pretty ripped up. Been dead about twelve hours."

Stryker has something he does called "the two-second

ponder." That means you collapse half an hour's worth of data and pointed questions and make the same decision that you would have made if you'd actually taken the thirty minutes to ponder it. I stood up and put my leather jacket on.

"Let's go."

16

When we got to the car, Doug slung the Kojak onto the roof and we flashed our way out of there at a conservative 45 MPH till we hit the edge of town, then boosted it to 80. It felt natural to be riding with him and I felt my commitment to him deepen just a shade.

The next thing I heard while we were screaming down the highway was Stryker's ninja litany in his own basso profundo coming from the place in my brain into which he had burned it years ago: "To influence the lives of men, one must remain outside the circle of forces that affect them."

The sensei had spoken. I took a psychological step back and remembered that Doug wasn't my cousin, I wasn't a cop, and I needed to be thinking about how to blow my cover in the most strategic way. Unconsciously, I placed my thumbs in the sixth kanji position of jen to effect balance and strength.

We got to the scene. It was a little north of town along the main spur for the railroad. An old house trailer had been abandoned there, stripped, and mostly ravaged by people and time. The victim had been found tucked under some of the sheet metal, where the buzzards had pointed her out to some fishermen heading up to the county lake. The dump site was close to Casey's estate.

Americans have a lot of funny ideas about death. We lost our national virginity during Nam when the five o'clock news showed all those sheltered middle-class folks what it was really like. The day *Time* magazine ran the cover that showed a small Vietnamese guy getting his head blown off, we all grew up some. And yet since then, the same media has produced murder and mayhem in thirty- and sixty-minute TV segments every day of the week, and the R-rated deaths are pretty sanitized. The visual medium also makes it odorless.

Real death smells. Especially when it's had a little time to naturally age in the elements. When I got out of the car and detected a twelve-hour-old dead body on the Missouri breeze, I remembered riding with a forensics team in Colorado on a house call. When we got to the house in question, they handed me a jar of Vicks and told me to stick some up into my nose. The coroner was in tow and he handed me a short crooked cigar that he called his secret weapon. It was an honorable-smelling Mississippi Crook. A great fishing cigar. Given the circumstances, it was welcomed. Even then, the smell of putrefaction was intense. Of course, that body had been in ninety-degree heat for nearly a week.

The estimated time of death on this Missouri evening

was only half a day, so it was not as hard on the nose as it was on the eyes. As promised, she was lying facedown. Half her clothes were gone, including the bra that had held the little drug pouch. The butter-soft leathers were blood-crusted ghosts of their former selves.

When the deceased had been duly photographed and turned over, her left breast was exposed and it bore a tattooed heart with Arnie's name inside it. The face in death was as vacant as it had been in life. She was pretty cut up and there were purposeful gunshot wounds to her head, her heart, and her crotch. Whoever did it didn't just want to kill her. They wanted to make a point.

I watched Doug work. He was good. He debriefed his officer and secured the scene. The officer didn't appear to notice me.

A second squad car pulled up, summoned from nowhere, and I could see from the guy's swagger that he didn't belong to Doug. He strolled up and just about threw me against the car with his eyes. He got testy with me.

"This is a crime scene, mister. What are you doin' here?"

"I was invited."

I was cool. He shot me a contemptuous look and walked over to talk to Doug and the other guy.

We took a lot of pictures, located evidence that we wanted to bag and send to the lab, and covered about half an acre around the site, scuffing for nothing in particular and finding our share of old cans, bottles, fast-food containers, and condoms, all unlikely to be related. Then we waited until the county coroner arrived to tell us what we already knew: She was dead. Doug shot a pointed look at his own officer as if to say "Be my second and keep an eye on Brock's goon." It was done in an eye blink. Then he walked over to me.

"I gotta find Arnie. He's gonna be a time bomb."

"You think Arnie did it?"

"Hell, no. But I think this is connected to the stuff that we were just talking about, and I think Arnie's part of it. The way he thinks, if you can call it that, he's damn sure going to try to avenge it. This is like ..."

"A telegram to someone?"

"Yeah, a telegram. Jesus, I'd give my eyeteeth to know where Brock was twelve hours ago."

I filed the comment. We took off for the biker bar.

17

We didn't speak in the car. There was no need. We made Geek's place in ten minutes and it was in full swing. Doug walked in like a man who'd had this problem before and the sound in the room changed. Nobody stopped doing what they were doing, but everyone was acutely aware that the Chief of Police from Richmond had arrived, was boldly invading their space, and was about to stomp in their shit.

I gotta hand it to Doug. He didn't miss a step as he moved directly to Arnie's seat at the bar and got right in his face.

"Arnie."

If Arnie had moved any slower, it would have been tan-

tamount to ignoring Doug altogether. He finally swiveled
on the bar stool.

"Well, if it ain't Goldilocks and his new sherpa. You're
a little out of your playground here, head pig. Whaddya
want?"

"Step outside, Arnie. I got something I need to tell you
in private."

"Hey, man. These are my people, my family. You got
anything to say, you can say it in front of them. So what
do you wanna say?"

Doug lowered his voice and the crowd didn't have
enough time to lower its own volume to accommodate the
change.

"Arnie, I don't want to break your arm to give you bad
news, but I will if I have to. Get your ass out into the
parking lot before I drag it out feet first."

Arnie was not a dummy. He sauntered across the bar
floor and kicked open the door like he was in charge. We
walked past the parked motorcycles, and when we were
far enough away, Doug rounded on him.

"It's about Slew."

Arnie looked mildly alarmed.

"Yeah. Well, where the hell is she? She's supposed to be
visiting a friend a hers. What have you done with her, pig?"

Doug's eyes blazed. "Shut the fuck up, y'little asshole.
She's dead, man. Someone killed her. We found her in a
field."

What happened next surprised me and I don't surprise
easily. Arnie stood there and looked as sick behind the eyes
as any man who has lost someone he loves.

His wail, when it came, was directed at God.

"Fuuuccccckkkkkeeeer!"

Doug stood his ground and watched Arnie double up
with pain. He was as dispassionate as a panther. He waited
for the wail to stop.

"Arnie, I got no reason to believe that you did it. But if I get even a rumor that you're taking your ass outta the county, I will throw it in jail faster than a crack of thunder. Suspicion of murder. Do you understand me?"

Mimi was coming toward us across the parking lot, swaying, I suspect, from whatever she was drinking too much of and responding to Arnie's wail. There were three ugly bikers standing under Geek's old awning watching it all.

When she got to the circle of three, Mimi pushed Arnie aside and lit into Doug. It was as if I weren't there. I was invisible to the she-lion protecting her raging infant from some predator.

"So what are you hassling Arnie about, Ketchum? Are you arresting him on some fucked-up charge you can't prove? Did you maybe want me to show you a good time so you'll be nice to us? We can just go on around back. Shit, who do you think you are comin' out here anyway? Go play pig in your own sty."

She spat and missed. The roundheels talked to the Police Chief as if she didn't care whether she lived or died or ended up in jail. I wanted to give her a good swift drop kick before she pushed him too far.

Arnie stared away trance-like, then finally reached out and absently touched her arm.

"Enough, Mimi. Slew is dead. She's dead. Ketchum says somebody murdered her. She's dead, Mimi. She's gone."

I have never seen anyone change that fast. From one altered state to another. She looked like a little girl who suddenly didn't know what the adults were saying. Arnie wasn't much help. He turned away in a kind of slow motion, saddled up, and roared off on the panhead.

Mimi looked from my face to Doug's and back again. I tried the gentle approach.

"Mimi?"

She looked at me but would not speak. She backed up slowly until she was under the awning, where the bikers gathered around her protectively. She crossed her arms across her body as if she were a child holding herself for comfort. I wondered how many times she'd had to do that when her mama worked the trailer court. She moved with the bikers back into the bar.

I had more to deal with than seemed possible.

18

We got back to the car and Doug radioed in.

"Put a tail on Arnie. If he looks like he's going to split town or if he looks too weird, take him down. I'm comin' in."

The officer at the other end didn't ask any questions. They called her Tackleberry because she was a shavetail, but she was also a cop's cop and the word would get out just like Doug wanted it. Brock had no influence over her, and Doug had earned her respect a long time ago when he hired her onto an all-male force in a town full of rednecks. I asked him to drive me back to my car and he did.

We didn't speak. I got into my car and took off into a black Missouri night. I could have stayed at the inn, but

Mimi's face kept floating up in front of me and I was very clear about the next step in the process.

I pulled up on her street, a few houses away from hers, and waited. About forty-five minutes later, I heard the sounds of a righteous chopper. One of Arnie's boys dropped her off at her doorstep. She slipped herself off the cycle and half-hugged her courier. When she walked into the house, she slammed the door and I had the impulse to leave well enough alone. She was safe. I could have sat there and made sure it was true without putting myself through the exercise of talking to her.

I never trust the first impulse, so I waited till the sound of the departing cycle was subliminal and then I abandoned the car. I walked to the door almost casually, but I could hear my heart beating a tattoo against the walls of my chest. It wasn't fear so much as it was apprehension. Women, no matter how much they deny it, are strange and crazy creatures, and I would rather tangle with a puma than face a woman in a weird head space.

I knocked on the door. She opened it. Not a puma but a wounded Bengal tiger and still drunk as a lord.

"Mimi?"

She narrowed her eyes and swayed a little trying to steady herself.

"Hey! Hopper-Farber-asshole. Things have just been wonderful around here since you hit town. Good to see you."

She spat the last words out as she backed into the house. In the dim recesses of the living room, she looked like a voodoo doll ready to curse me forever, her face in blue shadow, menacing. She was still unsteady on her feet.

"Mimi, listen."

"I don't have to listen. Slew is dead. Arnie sold her. I could have kept them both from it, d'you understand? Only I couldn't really because I..."

111

She started to fall under the weight of the alcohol, and I caught her in a hairbreadth and pulled her down on the couch. She whimpered against my shoulder. I kept my mouth shut and stroked her hair, feeling every muscle of her body tensed in some crazy protest against the night.

"Talk to me."

I whispered, not certain yet that she was able to say anything at all. She took a deep shuddering breath.

"Why talk, Hopper? Why try?"

Her voice was spent in a monotone of dead misery. I elected to wait.

I was rewarded with some snuffling and then soft crying and then the kind of sobs that human beings can't speak through. When it subsided, she sighed.

"So talk to me, Mimi. Slew is dead and it doesn't make any sense. Help me understand."

She raised her head as if to do battle but it didn't last long.

"Slew was ... special."

"How so? Maybe Arnie loved her, but her life with him couldn't have been much. She looked like she was half fried on drugs. I don't know why she died, but I also don't know why she was special."

Mimi was quiet, breathing steadily against my chest.

"Slew was the daughter of my mama's friend who died when Slew was a baby. Mama took her in. Me and Arnie and Slew all grew up together. When Slew was in third grade, they gave her some tests and said that she wasn't right. That she couldn't learn. They wanted Mama to put her in a state home. My mama couldn't support us except on her back but ... "

I listened to the tears again and I was quiet.

" ... but none of us were going to sit still for Slew being in a home. So she stayed."

"And then what happened?"

"We did okay. I was the smart one. I went to school on

a scholarship, and while I was gone, Arnie was drafted. He got out early because he said he was the sole support of the family. But while he was getting his orders to come home, Mama died. Arnie ended up coming back to take care of Slew. Meanwhile, I was in school learning what it meant to be 'developmentally delayed.' Her brain wasn't fried on drugs, Hopper. It's just the way she was born."

I thought back to her features, her differences, her slowness, and cursed the professionalism that allowed me not to feel what Mimi was feeling.

"What about Arnie?"

"He became a biker. Slew didn't much care. She didn't use drugs hardly ever, but she carried his. She just wanted to be where he was and stay close to him. He was . . . all she had left. By the time I came back, she was his lady. I didn't like it much at first, but then I thought . . . Oh, never mind."

"Never mind what, Mimi? We got nothing left to lose here. She's dead."

"Well, Arnie treated her pretty good until two years ago when he cut his deal. There's only one other person who Gaiters got off on more than me and it was Slew. Since then, Brock's guys pulled her in twice as much as me and Arnie didn't do a goddamned thing. He didn't kill her, Hopper. He couldn't have. But if he used her as a chip in his deal like I think he did, I'm going to kill him, go rot in the Missouri State Pen, and read books for the rest of my life."

She was hissing again, and then, just as quickly, she collapsed like some rag doll that had lost the support of the child who believed in her.

"Why didn't I kill him, Hopper? Why didn't I kill that knobby-kneed old fart with his bad breath and his sweaty hands? Why didn't I? I had lots of chances. Why didn't Arnie? Arnie coulda done it."

She was bereft. I stroked her hair and ran my hands

down the long slender muscles at her waist. When I cupped her behind, something in both of us stirred. There are some women who have a way of coming up from their grief that impassions their lovemaking, and Mimi was one of them.

I slid up to her breast and she moved her hands in all the right places, going steadily south. Clothes dropped like sunset and eventually we each cried out in voices not of sorrow and not of joy.

She slept then, like a soldier who had made it across a mine field, deserving safe harbor. I held her like a sentry doing his job and dreaming of easier duty.

19

I grabbed an afghan from an adjacent chair and covered us both. I tried to nap and failed. When I looked at the brass mantel clock with the fluorescent dial, the big hand was on the four and it was still black as pitch. The exhausted sister/harlot/lover still snored softly with her fists curled into her chest, the fine red hair splayed across her cheek and naked shoulder.

There are some men who come to live their lives with a pane of glass between their feelings and the rest of the world. I am one of them. We always see quite clearly through our shield, but the shield is there, relentlessly and of necessity. But I was touched by her. I was touched by her toughness and her bravery and her pain.

Still I wished I had found some other way to express it besides the quick, intense coupling on her antique couch. Men, when they are too moved to speak, resort to the only form of intimacy that the world uninhibitedly allows them. But I wasn't very comfortable.

My wife's face drifted up in that mist that accompanies the long-gone beloved. I still missed everything there was to miss about her, but I missed her most at times like this. I wanted to be able to reach out and touch her and say, "What now, babe? What do I do now?" She'd always had an answer.

But this was Richmond and that was a long time ago. I extricated myself carefully and tucked the afghan tighter around Mimi. I considered leaving her a note, but I wasn't sure what it could say. My clothes were hard to untangle and sort in the dark, but I looked respectable enough as I left the house.

A quick trip to the inn, where a steam and a Jacuzzi blitz revived me. The water pounded at the fatigue, and although I was tempted to just stay with the feeling of relief, I forced myself into reconnaissance mode. The foundation was beginning to crack. I had the names I needed, but not the chinks to start driving the wedges into yet. Somebody had made a big mistake as far as Slew was concerned. Either she'd found out too much from a too-drunk judge or it was a symbol. Either way it was likely to be the opening I needed to start making some of my favorite kind of moves—fast and rough. The fast part would require the services of Cochise since my alliances were already getting too ambivalent. Both Doug and Mimi.

Time was not on my side, but I suspected that if I could only get one of the team to crack, the rest would hurry in to turn on the others and save their own asses. At least I now had the whole roster. It was time to go steal a play book. To do that, I needed Cochise in the locker room. I toweled off and hit the phone.

The Richmond police and fire dispatcher, also the Mayor of neighboring Henrietta, answered the phone on the sixth ring. She had probably been in the squad anteroom making coffee. I asked for the Chief.

"Chief Ketchum speaking."

"Hopper, Chief."

"Yo, what's happenin'?"

"I think we both agree on the basics of what needs to be done. Now we have to figure out who does what to whom, when, where, and why. I think we got a short fuse here. I'm not useful as the mysterious stranger anymore, and I'm calling in a second. You got any problems with that?"

"Nope."

I was surprised that I didn't get any party-line resistance, but I also *wasn't* surprised because my intuition about this Police Chief was correct. He was more interested in getting things done than in playing it safe. I thought about Jake Barnum sitting at home in Colorado. Jake would have understood and been right in there grinning and throwing punches with us just to hear his knuckles pop. I pushed it a bit further.

"I'm worried that Mimi's next. Can you put someone on her for the time being?"

"Not real easy. The ones who won't spill it to Brock are mighty few for now and she moves around a lot. Seems to me you did a pretty good job of protectin' her last night, though. You think she needs more?"

The guilt hit again and it hurt, but there was no time for that now. I didn't like it much that Doug had staked out the house, but I understood why he'd done it. I selected "cheeky" as a response.

"Glad to see you're on the job, bro, but I'm not making any apologies. Do I get the protection or not?"

There was a pause to consider the implications.

"You got it."

"Doug?"

"Yeah?"

"I'd suggest that you cut Tackleberry loose for this duty."

"Okay. Call me with the plan."

"Where's Arnie?"

"No place special. Sitting in his little house seein' how drunk he can get. You got any more orders for me, asshole?"

"I wouldn't presume."

He hung the line up without saying good-bye, but I had what I wanted. I turned my attention to other matters.

I dialed up the Chinese restaurant in St. Louis that Jake had told me about. I got a very earnest employee who said that Little Brother's phone number could only be extended by a principal. I asked for the principal. She declined. I pressed it. She acquiesced.

I got the number but grudgingly. It was the Vocational Rehabilitation Division for the State of Missouri. He was hiding again in the belly of yet another bureaucratic beast. I suspected that in his spare time Little Brother was actually helpful to the crazies and the winos he counseled. Just as he was helpful to the worn-out drug strike forces caught in the useless endeavor of cutting back on America's propensity for substances and the grand capitalistic enterprises that they spawned. I talked to three secretaries before they could locate him. The last one was a peach. She was determined to find this anonymous vocational rehabilitation counselor simply because I'd asked her to and because she took her job seriously.

Several electronic switches were tripped and finally I had him.

"This is Don."

"Cochise?"

"I beg your pardon?"

He was a polite little sonuvabitch, and despite the fact that I knew that he recognized my voice and could see me in his mind's eye down to the most minute detail, he wasn't going to recognize me until I said more words and revealed some kind of extra proof that I was who I was.

"Knock it off, Little Brother. It's Hopper. Say good night, Gracie."

"Hey. Goo'night, Gracie. How the hell are you? I'm sorry man, it's just that—"

"Yeah, lemme guess, it's just that you happen to be involved in an investigation in which you're convinced that some guy is going to cut your balls off if you surface. Well, I ain't interested. It's your problem. I just want your body and your brain for a few."

"Must be you, Hopper. It's been a long time."

I heard a door slam and I could see him kicking it with a heavy boot and leaning over the public-sector, government-issue desk that suited him about as well as fur fits a cobra.

"Yeah. It's been a long time. What's been happening?"

"Not much. Did you hear the one about the guy who—"

"Later, my friend."

Cochise was a short-term catalog of every joke that ever hit the streets. He heard them. He spread them around. And then he went on to a new batch. Normally I would have listened to two or three, but I was in a hurry.

"Okay. No jokes. Tell me what's goin' on in Denver."

"Don't know. I've been in Richmond for the last few days."

"Virginia or Missouri?"

"Hey, I'm not applying for state assistance here, bro. Just your assistance. Quit asking so many questions and just listen."

"Jesus, whatever's happening is sure making you grumpy."

119

Jake Tanner

"You got it. Your kind of deal, bro. PCP, LSD, and real fancy lab-born designer stuff like Ecstasy. I think it's a big operation feeding the K.C. family empire for sure, possibly a whole lot more. The lab is probably near here and well funded—and well protected by a gaggle of biker/runners and half a police force that the conspiracy owns. If you can get inside, find the lab and some hard evidence, I suspect that we could have us some unconventional fun with a capital *K*."

"Kickass, huh? Okay, I'm yours. Don't start it without me. I feel a hangnail coming on and I still got two weeks of sick leave left for this year. If that's not enough, I can always call in well and use some vacation."

"Why don't you get a real job, man?"

"And lose all these benefits? Where you hidin'?"

"The Elms in Excelsior."

"Well, you've either gotten into little old ladies or you've turned more hedonistic than the last time we met. Who is she?"

"Cut it out, you disrespectful half-breed. What's your ETA?"

"Six o menos."

"No escort. See you there."

It's a long way across Missouri.

I half expected him to come roaring up in his classic red 'Vette, but instead he'd chosen a tasteful navy Saab. He arrived too fast. It meant that he'd arrived by private air and already decided on the beginnings of his cover story. God knows, he usually drives a battered silver Datsun with a broken odometer.

It was good to see him. The friend at court. He sauntered into the bar—Aztecs have always compensated for their stature with a saunter—and inclined his head about half an inch. That was as much of a hello as I was going to get. I was reminded of Stryker's theory that most heroes are very shy people who make up for their lack of sociability by doing brave things.

"Well, Hopper, had your high colonic for the day yet?"

"No, but I did get a schvitz. Let's go grab a steam and I'll bring you up to date."

A split second after we stepped into the hall, and with little warning, I was flat on the floor as a consequence of his sudden impulse to show me his new martial arts trick. He let me up as quickly as he'd thrown me and laughed like hell. He does it about twice a year and I always allow it because his intention is so benign. There's something about our relationship that reminds me just enough of high school to make me trust him. Rituals can be very comforting.

"All right, hot dog. Now that that's out of the way, let's get serious here."

We cranked up the steam, doffed the towels, and opened the book to page one. The conspiracy had begun anew.

20

He listened to the whole story before commenting. "So, Hopper, all you want me to do is find the lab and connect it to these hotshots?"

"Sounds like you think it's going to be easy."

"It'll take me a day or two. I have to work up some enthusiasm and get inside. But it seems to me there's fun stuff we could do on this one."

"Such as?"

"Well, Hopper, you know how I hate violence, but we could try a little creative rough stuff since we're so far out in the boonies and nobody's looking. Taking them out might be an option. Then we wouldn't have to leave them to the unpredictability of our honorable legal system.

Y'know, sort of innocent until pronounced dead."

"Yeah, your abhorrence of violence makes the Godfather look like Liberace. Sorry. No big hammers anticipated on this one."

"So what's to stop them from putting the lab somewhere else?"

"Disclosure, I hope. No public official can get past a scandal these days. The press will fry all of them."

"What press? This county's got no fucking press! And first they gotta get wrapped up tighter than a goddamned mummy. Then they gotta get arrested, and if that's not enough, they gotta get convicted. Those guys'd draw two years suspended and get to do some 'community service.' Seems to me one of these guys could get loose on insufficient evidence. Especially McCain. I'll do whatever you want, but I think you're making a mistake if you think truth and justice will prevail on this one."

Little Brother was being his righteous self and it annoyed me because I knew he was right.

"So what makes you think that finding the chemist who's running the lab won't yield a willing witness for the State?"

"We're talking odds, Hopper. You wanna take the chance, we'll take the chance. But I'm into Colombian death squads myself."

"We don't have enough data to make that decision now. Just find out which ear we need to blow into to get both the lab and probable cause. Who are you this time around?"

"Lance Livermore, yuppie degenerate."

"I don't think Lance Livermore will play in Richmond, bro."

"The name is irrelevant. 'Larry' will do for the druggies because they don't care if you have a last name. For public presentations I'll use Covington. Trust me on the degenerate yup routine. I practically do this for a living, y'know."

"Fair enough. You need anything else from me?"

"Not right now. But think about my proposition, play out some fantasies on this one. I'll respect your limits, but you may need to keep reminding me."

He stood up and withdrew some black sunglasses from his jacket pocket. They had one of those fancy cords attached so he could hang them around his neck. His sweater was classic. He changed his posture slightly, donned the glasses, and I was looking at Larry Covington, degenerate yup. He saluted and left to do God knows what. Little Brother is not someone you need to brief on where to move next.

I called Mimi. She wasn't home or she wasn't answering. I called Ketchum and set up a meeting at his office. At this point, it served my purposes to make Brock's boys a little nervous about Jim Farber.

21

The police station was in the City Office Building. The door was on the north end next to the fire department driveway. I checked in with the dispatcher at the information window, told her who I was and something of what I was about. She called Doug on the intercom to check it out and let me through the security door into the inner sanctum.

Ketchum looked comfortable in his own chair.

"Get the door, Farber."

I shut it behind me and settled into an ancient decaying black-vinyl bucket that had probably been Brock's desk chair. Odds on this new Chief had furnished his own.

"So where's your second?" Doug asked.

"On the job and undercover by now. I doubt that he'll have to do anything overt enough to get arrested, but if one of Brock's guys comes in with a short, yuppie-looking guy with salt-and-pepper hair, let him escape, would you?"

"Pretty decent-size ego you got there, Hopper. I oughtta have my head examined for gettin' involved with you. What's the plan?"

"My guy doesn't need a bunch of legal wherewithal to do his thing. I want the lab and the guys who back it. Any objections?"

"So what the hell do you expect me to do while all this fancy shit is going on? Stand by? It's hard to look like a police chief with your head so far up your ass that you have to peek out your navel to maintain your sense of direction."

"You don't look to me like a guy who stands by real well," I said. "In addition to putting a tail on Mimi, is there any way we can keep an eye on Luther Brock?"

"Not without hiring someone else to do it. And I generally need to get the accounting office at City Hall to sign off on that. Not real likely, Hopper."

"Hire someone you trust. My checkbook."

"Damn, you're a piece of work."

"Yeah, that's what my mentor always said."

There was a knock on the door followed by an immediate entry. The Assistant Chief said he needed to be briefed. What he really needed was to satisfy his curiosity about his boss's guest. Doug backed him out of the room and closed the door behind him. His second-in-command had looked pained that he wasn't to be included in the conversation to follow. I suspected him to be one of the pipelines to Brock.

Doug's office was next to the squad room. It was a good working office, cramped but tidy. No windows. Large steelcase desk. Well-worn upholstered chair. Last generation's

Unisonic calculator. Small clock radio. Digital. There were a few code and procedure books and documents. Five volumes of Missouri State Statutes, a volume of Code of Ordinances, City of Richmond, a volume of the Missouri Criminal Code, four texts from the FBI National Academy. It was sparsely papered in law-enforcement certificates, but the ones that were there were framed and hung on the wall behind the desk. One from the Bureau of Narcotics and Dangerous Drugs, one that was a National Academy of Firearms award, another a private pilot's license. A coffee cup, probably from his kids, said WORLD'S GREATEST POLICEMAN. Cops' tools.

The dispatch office was across the hall. The squad room and watch commander's office were down the hall. That, plus a small restroom, a closet-turned-coffee-room, and a small evidence locker wrapped it up. But they did have the whole basement, and a walk-in basement at that.

While Doug was out, my eyes poked around on his desktop. The usual shift reports, warrants, extradition papers, and APBs were in neat little stacks. Open on the far side of the desk was an investigation report from the State Fire Marshall marked CONFIDENTIAL. There was something shiny under the calculator cover. My curiosity overwhelmed me. I peeked. It was a stainless-steel Smith and Wesson 9mm semiautomatic, model 669, with one round jacked into the magazine and the safety off. There were twelve more rounds in the clip of that one, and it was neatly arranged on top of his "Success" appointment book to point about heart high at the guest chair. An old cop trick. Let them watch the one on your hip while you drop them with another. I hoped it was nothing personal.

As the cover dropped over the gun, the door opened.

"Sorry that took so long," Doug said, coming back into the room. "Technically, he has a right to know what I have no intention of telling him. He's Brock's."

127

Bingo.

"Well, where do we sit?" I asked.

"I'm okay with it so far. Concerned about your sidekick, though. I think time's short, Hopper. I'll get Brock covered."

"Thanks."

"Keep in touch."

"You got it."

Somehow mentioning my sidekick led back to the dilemma that Little Brother had raised. Could we really get the system to do these guys or did we need a little more outlaw in our approach? I decided to discuss it with the master. From a pay phone. It was only two in the afternoon in the Baja, so I opted for his house, where I imagined his intellectual siesta to be taking place. I used my credit card and was rewarded with Lucia, the housekeeper.

"Diga!"

She had the thin, soprano voice of the elderly. I suspect that Lucia had been a beauty in her twenties, handsome in her thirties, and declining by her forties under the weight of hard work and poverty. She went to work for Stryker when she was in her sixties and she had a job for life. She missed spots on the crystal and he wiped them off himself. Nobody knows whether Stryker had a mother—I certainly couldn't imagine it—so Lucia was about as close as Stryker had probably gotten to having some filial attachment in his unusual life.

"Buenas tardes, hermosa. Donde esta el maestro?"

"Ah, Señor Rana. Como estas, hijo? De donde llamas?"

"Del estado de Mizzuri."

"Aye, muy lejos. Voy pronto. Momentito."

She clanked the phone down on the small antique table on which it customarily rests and went to fetch Dr. Stephens.

"Hopper." It was a statement, not a greeting.

"The very same. I've got a problem."

"I trust it's not a personal one."

"You trust correctly. I have handily blown about half of my real-estate cover, so I pulled in an operative. He raises the following question. If the conspiracy is as thick as we think it is and the system is as thick-headed as we believe it to be, can we really get all of them by the book?"

"Not a stupid question from an operative, but I am dismayed that you haven't provided your own answer. Of course, you can't get them all by the book. Has your life been so pleasant lately that you've lost your ability to think on the edge?"

"And what license do I have under our present agreement with the Foundation, Professor? This isn't Southeast Asia. This is Missouri, and the DEA is at the other end of this matter. What would Burroughs say if he knew his money was being used to rid the world of some small-town *narcotraficantes?*"

"I see no reason for him to find out. Besides, there are many kinds of death besides the final rattle. Anything else, bullfrog?"

"Yeah, how's the fishing?"

"Consistently superb, as you well know."

He hung up on me. I can reliably get him to do so by making small talk on the phone. Makes him crazy.

The dilemma was starting to make *me* a little crazy. I am no stranger to another's death by my hand. Most of it I accomplished with government permission a long time ago. I didn't like it much. It is the last resort when the fragile ties that bind the human community together are broken by declared war or other violence. What I wanted in this situation was not necessarily the death of the perpetrators but justice for the victims. Mimi's face, contorted by pain and rage, drifted up in front of my eyes. And Caitlin's. Always Caitlin's.

I went back to the inn to wait for a call from Cochise. When I arrived, the message light on the phone was blinking merrily and I called the front desk expecting to hear a pseudonym that I could identify as Little Brother.

"My message light is on. I'm in Room Two fifty-three."

"One moment, sir."

She put me on hold and it seemed like a long time, but I'm an impatient man.

"Yes, sir, a message came in at noon from a man named Arnie. The switchboard operator says she hopes the number is right because he wasn't speaking very clearly and she had to ask him to repeat it several times."

I took the number with some disgust. It wasn't that I disapproved of Arnie as much as that I liked Mimi more than I cared to admit. And for all I knew, Arnie was one of the scumbuckets. It wasn't clear to me how he knew where I was, but maybe he'd called the Rose Court first and put two and two together. There aren't that many places to stay in Richmond. I dialed the number.

22

The phone rang a long time.

"Hello."

Sounded like him, but I wanted to hear more.

"Is Arnie there?"

"Thizz Arnie."

"This is Jim Farber returning your call."

"Cut the crap, Hopper. Mimi's here and she looks like a piece of fuckin' dog meat. It's your fault and I'm fixin' to be the dog catcher. Case you don't know, we shoot 'em out here to keep 'em from crowdin' up the pound. For some reason, she wants to talk to you before I come mess you up. Said to tell you that Brock's boys took her to the woods out by the county lake and beat the living shit out of her. She played dead and they left her. She said you'd know what to do. She can't even talk right, man. They busted her jaw and kicked her stomach in and it's all because of you. Just like Slew. I know it, man. I can just feel it."

He was screaming into the phone and I was selecting the words that would get him to stop screaming. I pitched my voice much lower than the lowest tone that I ought to be able to reach, and I was as menacing as a water moccasin because I was fed up with him.

"Arnie, you listen to me. You are a two-bit biker creep and you sold your old lady down the river when you gave her to Gaiters. You'd sell your sister to the Devil, too, if it would keep your own sweet ass out of the stir. If you don't get her to the hospital now, I'm coming over to do it myself and to rip your fucking face off. Trust me, little man."

I heard the phone hit the hook on the other end, but he'd do it. The half-crazed half-brother would do it.

I lit into the phone as if it were Brock's hide and called the Richmond P.D. I got Doug on the line and ranted a bit.

"So, lawman. The saga continues. I just got a call from Arnie. They got to Mimi, but she's still alive, no thanks to your friggin' half of the police force. This one's on you, my friend. Maybe I was the fool to get involved with you instead of the other way around. Well, it's all mine now. If I can't trust you, I can't use you. Go write some parking tickets."

"Now, just a goddamned minute, Hopper. I got a Raytown officer who was doing us a favor in the hospital now because of a very suspicious auto accident that occurred while he was tailing your little girlfriend. I don't need you to tell me how to do my job and I don't like your attitude. I may not be up to full power on this force, but I can still run a stranger's ass out of town whenever I want to. Or I can call Ron Gable and nail you and whoever hired you. You got that?"

I backed up and cursed the temper that had gotten me

into a million scrapes when I was a kid. I had to assuage
the Chief's pride or lose a valuable ally. I lowered my voice
and spoke with a harnessed tongue.

"You really don't want to do that, and you know it.
Besides, you might run me out of town, but you couldn't
get to my team with a 'Q' clearance and a battalion of
Rangers."

He lowered his voice as well, and we each remembered
that we were on the same side of this shootout.

"Maybe not, but I'm not taking orders, Hopper. Where
the hell is your guy, anyway? This thing is about to come
unglued."

"I haven't heard from him and I'm going to go looking.
Where the hell is Brock?"

"Sitting in the picture window of his goddamned living
room with an off-duty from Northtown staring at him
through binoculars. Any other stupid questions?"

"Yeah. Why the hell does anyone want to become a cop?"

I hit the door on the run with the Colt and the lock picks.
I got to Arnie's house in about twelve minutes, and the
red van that served the fire department as an ambulance
was just turning out of the long driveway onto Garner.
The drive was halfway between Warner and Black Diamond, tucked between a dilapidated two-story coal-mine
Victorian and the projects. I probably would have blown
by it without the ambulance. I sent good thoughts with
her and went to his door. No answer. I assumed he was in
the ambulance prepared to lie his ass off to the hospital
admissions clerk.

I took out my favorite lock pick and I was into Arnie's
little house faster 'n most folks could find the right key on
their key ring. Ketchum was right. Arnie had been spending a lot of time trying to see how drunk he could get. Or
how stoned. It was one step up from a shack. Half early-
fifties vacation trailer and half frame add-on. The porch

was piled with car and motorcycle parts, and a Confederate flag hung from the eave. Slew was apparently a homebody because there were little replicas of their colors embroidered on pillows on the ratty couch. Overall, however, the place was a stinking mess with empty tequila bottles sitting mutely next to overflowing ashtrays of cigarette butts and roaches. There were fast-food bags and empty pizza boxes on the table. A few bits of rotting food.

All places can be assigned to some metaphor and this one looked and smelled like a backed-up toilet. I started to hunt in the sewage.

In the bedroom that Arnie and Slew must have shared, I found an old poster of Big Brother and the Holding Company, a faded banner from Richmond High School that said GO, SPARTANS, GO, and a lot of denim clothing flung onto chairs, the bed, and the floor. There was a plain double bed, a small bureau, and a closet with next to nothing in it. Over the bureau was a picture of the club in full dress, and next to it a picture of the man's family when he and it were young. Arnie looked like a young, rawboned dolt. Slew looked like a waif, and Mimi and her mama looked very similar. I turned away.

I checked the usual places for contraband. The inside of the toilet tank. The top of the oven, the floorboards. It was clean. I saw a keychain with a miniature Michelin tire lying on the kitchen table. With the pick, I flipped open the tire at the hubcap and was rewarded with some powder that was, according to my tongue, nothing more than bar coke. The kind you buy when it's late and you want something for the road. A small stash, but a stout one. No big deal. I was about to split when I saw the breakfront.

A breakfront is what used to be known as a china cabinet. It's supposed to hold plates and glasses and knickknacks. Arnie's breakfront held a few chipped pieces of Melmac and a shelf or two of books. Mostly trash. Except for something that looked like a ledger. Now, drug dealers don't use ledgers. They use computers or nothing at all. Nonetheless, I opened the glass door to the cabinet and pulled out the stiff-spined book. The most recent entries were scrawled versions of what looked to be descriptions and numbers for car parts. Most of them were high-end. They had prices attached. There wasn't much else of interest for twenty or thirty pages, just more of the same. And then I found a name of sorts. "McC's used," it said. Ten blank pages after that it said, "McC's shipped," followed by some more entries of car parts. It had to be McCain. It had to at least mean that Arnie and his squad were doing something with cars and McCain had something to do with it.

Cars and drugs just might go together in this county. I ripped off the ledger. I was pissed at Cochise for his absence and his silence although that's what I expected of most good undercover guys. I left Arnie's little hole and went hunting.

23

The steel rod that anchors my ass to the top of my head was stiffening now. I was linear and singular. I was real tired, once again, of the banality of evil. I drove the Thunderbird like it was a fighter plane, and I landed at Geek's without even thinking about it.

By the time I hit the door, I was calm. I walked up to the bar and marveled at how empty the whole room was. The word was out. Something was amiss. My yuppie operative wasn't here. I started to approach Geek.

"Gimme a beer, Geek."

"Fuck you."

"Excuse me?"

"Fuck you and get out of my bar."

I raised my hands in the classic "no weapons" sign and vacated the bar stool. I got crusty looks from the three bikers sitting at the back table.

I cruised the four bars in town from the Hideaway to Ethridges and couldn't find him. I called the only hospital listed in the Richmond telephone book.

"Excuse me. I wonder if you could connect me with Mimi Curtis."

"Is she an employee or a patient, sir?"

"She's a patient who probably arrived by ambulance about ninety minutes ago."

"One moment, please."

I waited again and my trapezius-muscle screws took a few more turns.

"We have no one here by that name, sir."

"Is there another hospital in town, miss?"

"No, sir. There are a few clinics. Was your friend just sick or what?"

"My friend got beaten up. Have you admitted any woman in the last couple of hours with multiple bruises and abrasions?"

"Um, no, sir. We did deliver two babies, however."

"Yeah, well, thanks."

He'd admitted her under an assumed name and the switchboard operator didn't know about it, or he hadn't admitted her at all.

It was a hard, cold Missouri night.

24

I went back to the inn again feeling like a Canadian goose who'd lost its navigational ability. I was off course and ornery. The phone rang and I picked it up like it was the Savior's cross.

"Yes."

"I'm checking in."

"Bloody well time. I looked for you. That was a fruitless exercise."

"Yeah. So?"

"So what have you got for me?"

"Just preliminary stuff, man. There are more little redneck pushers in this part of the world than you can shake a stick at. They told me some about Arnie, the man, and they told me some about Lavelle, but it isn't anything you don't already know. I need to tell you the rest of it in person. Sit tight."

"Welded to the chair. But I'm not used to having any help, and this whole gig is making me feel like an accountant with a broken pencil."

"I hear you. Soon, bro."

It took him exactly thirteen minutes to get to the inn. I know. I counted. I heard the tasteful Saab screech into the parking lot. I poured myself a Bombay and waited for my field hand to bring me a bushel of intelligence.

He walked in five minutes later wearing a T-shirt, jeans, and dirty red Converse high-tops. He quietly said that he'd stopped off in his room to change because eight hours in any uniform gave him a rash. I was in no mood for one-liners, but I listened without comment because it was his lead.

"So what else did you get?" I asked him.

"An interesting cat who says that he can deliver Methylene Dioxy Methamphetamine to wherever I want in no time at all. The price is lower than it is in St. Louis. I paid under market for a sample. You owe me a little for job-related expenses. It's good stuff. Lab quality before it gets stepped on." He cocked an eyebrow. "I tested it. Not bad. You could sell it to stockbrokers at half the strength."

He leered but his eyes were clear, so I let it go.

"The great yuppie designer drug Ecstasy, huh?" I said. MDMA. "So you got a minnow. Did he know anything about the friggin' aquarium?"

"I'd bet on it. He's a weak-chinned little shit but probably whole enough to know who's connected to his pipeline. We got a meeting later tonight. You got ten thousand dollars with you?"

"I got five thousand in real bills. The rest is funny money."

139

"Give me all you got. The worst that happens is that I'm established. We'll get it back. But I'm probably going to need to give a little more before I receive. How much more can you get?"

"As much as you need to do it right."

I handed him the money and he counted it in quick movements like a cashier at the two-dollar window. He finished and pocketed it in a black wallet the size of a savings bond.

"Where and when are you meeting him?" I asked.

"Somewhere known as the nigger bar. I got the address and ignored the politics. I don't hear that word without remembering Big Billy Davis."

I remembered Billy, too. He was a black Colorado Sheriff's Deputy, a road sergeant in an affluent, mostly white suburban community. One night I watched him take down a black man and wrap him around the squad car so hard he looked like a Dali watch. Eyes blazing, he called him a nigger. I said, "Jesus, Billy. If I did that, they'd call it police brutality." He grinned and said that the black dude was a nigger and knew it and that "nigger" had nothing to do with the color of your skin. It had to do with who you were and how you went about it. Billy wasn't a racist. He was a behaviorist. Little Brother had been riding shotgun that night for the hell of it. He remembered and so did I.

"Later, Cochise. Work fast and careful, okay?"

"Maybe. Check for messages."

25

Mimi dominated my attention like an outstanding debt. I hit the blacktop on 10, hung a right at the light onto Spartan Drive, slid to a stop behind the flagpole on the gravel circle, got out of the car, and strolled into the Ray County Memorial Hospital and Health Department about fifteen minutes later. I looked like I knew where I was going, and I stuck my head in a dozen doors before I found her. Arnie wasn't there. She was. The chart said Mrs. Arnold Kardis. No insurance. It was a small town and they'd admitted her anyway. She was asleep.

Her left eye looked like a black-and-blue football. Her head was bandaged and her arm was in a cast. Her upper lip was fat as a Southern watermelon, and her one free fist was clenched and drawn up against her chest like it had been when I'd left her two days ago. There was another bed in the room and it was empty.

I moved to her side and pressed on her unbroken wrist. It was a method my rangy rancher father told me about when I was nine years old. He had a soldier buddy who used to wake him up that way in the Army. It was gentle and effective and usually followed by an orange for breakfast. She awakened without a sound, just as my father had.

I put my fingers to my lips and asked for silence. She reached up to touch me. The brave red hair stuck out of the gauze wrap, and I wanted to make love to her again right then to take the pain away. We desisted. At least I desisted. She was probably in too much agony to give a damn.

"Mimi?"

"Aah?"

She tried to speak, but her mouth was mincemeat and it hurt to watch her. I had never met Luther Brock, but his face was beginning to set up in my imagination as cruel and unusual. Soon, I hoped, it would be rearranged by the hands at the end of my arms.

"Mimi, I heard it was Brock's boys. Is that right?"

She nodded.

"Can you identify them?"

She nodded again.

"Is there anything else you can tell me?"

Her eyes filled with tears then and she closed them while she shook her head no.

I didn't buy it, but I didn't press her either. There would be time later to ask all the hard questions. I kissed her forehead and left. I smiled at both nurses on my way out.

I called Ketchum from the pay phone in the lobby.

"This is Chief Ketchum."

"No shit. I'm at the hospital. You need to cover her here. If they figure it out, and they will, she'll need the protection or she's dead. She can also give you a positive I.D. This hospital is a sieve."

"I'll take care of it."

26

I went back to the inn understanding that it was to be a no-sleeper. I was a tapdancer, rapping out percussion with my feet, thinking too fast to record. Little Brother called at four A.M. It startled me out of a pattern search and I was on it before the first ring quit.

"Hello."

"There's an all-night trucker's diner about a mile north of the inn on the right-hand side of the road."

"On my way."

Whatever it was had motivated the kid to call me in the middle of the night and demand my presence. I didn't think that he was inviting me for chicken fried steak in a rustic environment. I was not disappointed.

When I got there, the restaurant was empty and he was nowhere to be seen. An old guy came up to my table and asked me what I wanted. I ordered a grapefruit, which he claimed not to have, and a cup of coffee, which he brought quickly and easily.

I drink my coffee black and I gave up smoking a long time ago. There's not much left to do with your hands but sip and wait. About halfway through the cup of mud-java, the chrome-and-glass door swung open and there was Lance or Larry or Cochise, depending on your point of view. Most people look half-dead at four-thirty in the morning, but he looked as though he'd just walked out of his morning shower after a two-mile run. Almost.

He slid into the seat.

"Hey."

"Yeah, Cochise. Whatcha got?"

"About four hundred square feet of outbuilding in a wooded section of a reputable ranch. Equipment is state-of-the-art. I didn't meet the caretaker because my tour guide was jailbait and I promised to drive her home."

"So where's this piece of real estate?"

"The rear end of Casey's spread."

"Who's the jail bait?"

"Name of Vivian. Nice Irish Catholic girl. Siphons off some of her old man's drug operation. He's too preoccupied to notice and she's too stupid to keep her rebellious adolescent mouth shut."

"Vivian Casey."

"Yeah. Nice kid. Real crazy. Wanted to buy some 'ludes."

"Did you have to sell her any?"

"Please. I slipped her a couple of No-Doz and charmed her with my older-man routine. Fed her a couple of beers and she got loose about the circumstances of her home life. We took a ride."

"So what's the mark on your neck? I met Vivian Casey. She can't be more than fifteen."

He snorted. "Cost of doing business. Let me up, man. I found her at the depot down the road a piece, wound around a very dark person. I left her off safe and sound. She's going to need some help later. I'll see that she gets it."

I thought about Casey's little girl in training to be the lady of the manor and playing the family version of double agent instead. I saw a dark-haired, pretty high-school girl leaving a bad-girl mark of revenge on the neck of an older man who she believed to be a drug dealer like her sainted Irish daddy. I wanted to gag and I couldn't.

"So what else?"

"The lab looks like any other toolshed on a farm. Probably been there for years. Only the insides have changed."

"So you didn't meet the caretaker. Did you see him at least?"

"Yeah. He's a bearded dildo who looks like he'd be a computer repairman if he weren't a chemist. He was mixing a batch of something and picking his nose. No social skills. We didn't stay long. I didn't want any surprises."

"Anything else?"

"Maybe."

"You gonna tell me about it or do I have to lay a bill on you, Little Brother?"

"Well, it's none of my business, but the jacket that was thrown in the corner of the shed was colors. Serpentine. I haven't seen them since Atlanta."

"Suggestions?"

"Let's blow the motherfucker up."

27

There were three scenarios to factor in this algebraic, multinational hometown mess. The first was that we would simply blow the lab up and split town to await a reaction from the powers that used to be. That was the most naked negotiating tool. It might yield some Kansas City big-timers complete with a grand-jury show, but it would take a long time and in the interim some entrepreneur would start moving into the market niche.

The second option was to disable the principals and let the DEA and the Richmond police do the mop-up on the facilities and the market. Of course, disabling the principals would muddy the legal waters, and there was no telling whether the DEA and the local policemen had the wherewithal to wrap it up.

The third scenario belonged to Little Brother. Blow the motherfucking lab up *and* disable the principals. After that the DEA and the cop shop could take next steps or rock back on their haunches because the immediate problem would be gone. The deed would be done. One way or the other.

I get stubborn sometimes. I could have called the Foundation for policy. I could have called Doug Ketchum for strategy. I could have talked to my operative for tactics. Instead I paced and sweated my way toward a sign.

The phone rang. I answered and the sign was delivered by the bass voice of a fully challenged police chief in a backwater district. I listened like it was a Bible reading. His voice was efficient and matter-of-fact.

"That you, Hopper?"

"Yeah."

"Brock's gone. Facedown in a ditch under a few pounds of lime and not enough dirt."

"When?"

"Found him an hour ago. The corpse is pretty fresh."

"How?"

"His throat was slit. Not by someone who was new to it. They also cut off his nuts and stuffed 'em in his mouth."

"Arnie?"

"Probably."

"So?"

"So nothing. Whatever is going to happen is going to happen in the next twenty-four hours."

"Agreed. We're going to move."

There was a pause at the other end of the phone and I could feel the lawman struggling with himself. He sighed then.

"Let me know."

"No problem."

We broke the connection and I rang Little Brother's room.

"This is Larry."

"This is Hopper. Move. Now. Take what you can for evidence and don't leave anything else standing at the site."

"Done. Thanks."

28

At two-thirty A.M., an out-building on the Casey farm turned into a pretty pillar of flame, but not before two guys in black coveralls pocketed the evidence and set it up to look like an accident. I knew one of them. I might never know the other. I didn't need to. There were no casualties. When Casey flew up the road in an old Ford pickup at three-thirty A.M., there was nothing there but the volunteer fire department guys clucking while they put out the chemical fire. They'd been alerted by some kids in the midst of a sexual experiment on the back forty.

The firemen contained the blaze and chose not to offer an opinion on how it had started. By Friday morning, the last embers were dead and the K.C. families and their minions were out a few big ones in capital improvements, millions in product. Cochise checked in about an hour later.

"So, Little Brother, you got the soot out of your eyes yet?"

"I got a lot of bad shit in this hotel room that we took before we leveled the shack."

"Who's we?"

"None of your goddamned business."

"Anyone I know?"

"No comment."

"Where's the chemist?"

"About four feet from me, looking glum. He's a little tied up at the moment."

"Just stand by."

"No problem. The chemist has got primo professional secrets that he's willing to share to keep me from putting my cigarette out in his eye."

"Stay on it."

"Try and keep me off it."

I would have chuckled, but I was planning the next move.

Brock's death had hit the one Richmond paper in a big way. They were doing a soppy retrospective of the old Chief. It was the first time I'd seen his face. It was grizzled, lined, and cagey. Graying hair and mean set to his mouth. As cruel and unusual as I had imagined it. Ketchum was quoted as saying that the City of Richmond owed ex-Chief Brock a debt of gratitude. Somehow the same paper managed to pawn off the burning of the outbuilding on Casey's ranch as a routine accidental fire. No suspicion of arson. And somehow the admission of Mimi Curtis to a local hospital with audacious wounds was not considered newsworthy at all.

Three things happened in rapid succession. The first two were surprises and the third was an opportunity. The first jolt came from Cabo San Lucas. Stryker called. It made me uncomfortable. Stryker takes calls. He doesn't make them.

29

To what do I owe the honor, Doc?"

"I'm just the messenger, Hopper. Lawless called."

"And?"

"And his contact says that Brock's death has not gone unnoticed in the DEA community."

"Jesus Christ, am I about to be descended upon by the vigilante forces? Did they finally get interested enough to get off their duffs? Timing couldn't be worse, Stryker. Can Lawless's guy hold them off?"

"How long?"

"A week."

"Possible, not probable. What else do you need to get it done?"

"I was exploring that very question when you called. I don't know exactly what Brock's role was in this operation, but I know that while McCain, Casey, and Gaiters still breathe, the problem isn't solved."

"No lethal force, Hopper."

"How about nonlethal force?"

"What did you have in mind?"

"A long-term disability."

"All of them?"

"Most of them."

"How?"

"I'm going to deal them a drug they've never had in their inventory before."

"So they'll be hoist by their own petard? Interesting."

"Yup. Instant karma."

"Proceed, then." That was as close as Stryker ever got to saying that he actually liked one of my ideas. To pronounce something "interesting" was high praise indeed.

"Tell Sergio to get ready. We'll need a mule on this one. It's not likely that we can get the goods locally, and he'll need to arrange for the diplomatic pouch."

"Signal when ready."

I turned the new model of destruction upside down and examined it from several angles. A plan, according to Stryker, should meet a number of criteria. It should be elegant. It should be ethically sound. It should avoid unnecessary deaths. It should be practical to implement. Check. Check. Check. Check.

The only glitch left to be resolved was how to get them in the same place at the same time and how to administer the quasi-lethal potion. I had an idea about the substance, but I needed a consult with my operative before I set Cordero in motion.

I was just about to go look for him when the second jolt came in the form of a knock on the door. I opened it and I was staring at Doug Ketchum out of uniform.

"We got an additional problem, Hopper," he said.

"Well, step into my office and let's see if we can wrestle it to the ground."

He looked out of place in the hotel chair. He leaned back and shook his head.

"What's the matter, Doug? Is this case getting too crazy?"

"Too crazy by half. I got an anonymous tip this morning. Right after the paper hit the stands."

"About what?"

"Young Joe McCain. He runs his daddy's used-car lot out on Highway Ten at the west end of town."

"What did the squeal have to say?"

"She made a lot of allegations about hot cars, drugs, and bikers being in bed with Brock and the Mayor."

"She?"

"Yeah, but she was talking through a towel or something and I didn't recognize the voice. It sounded young. It wasn't Mimi. It might have been one of the biker chicks getting scared about what's been coming down, but I doubt it."

I could sit tight and just let the Chief try to make his own case or I could deliver the little ledger book and Arnie's ass would be in jail. The question was whether I wanted Arnie's ass in jail or whether he was more useful to me on the streets as a loose agent who wasn't yet aware of how close we really were.

"Do you have enough to bring in Arnie on suspected homicide?"

"That ain't the question, friend. The question is whether Gaiters and Lavelle would take the chance of having Arnie go through an interrogation. If a warrant were issued, he'd probably have an accident on the way in. And I doubt that I'll be seein' any warrant."

"And if I provided some material evidence that Arnie is involved in the McCain hot-auto operation, what would

Lavelle and Gaiters do? They'd be at risk for judicial censure later if they ignored it."

The man's head snapped up and he glared at me. There isn't any other word to describe it. He was pissed. He bellowed.

"Jesus *Christ,* whose side are you on, Hopper? What the hell else are you sitting on that I don't know about and can't use because it was seized illegally?"

I owed him part of the truth. I lowered my voice.

"At the moment, I'm sitting on several pieces of material evidence against Casey, one piece of material evidence against Arnie, and one material witness against the whole gang. I'm guilty of illegal search and being an accessory to arson and illegally detaining a known criminal drug chemist who under our crazy laws can probably claim kidnapping. So what the hell else is new, Doug? That's the way undercover is played. When you signed off on me and my operative, you signed off on all the rest of it. You trust me or you don't. That's always what it comes down to, isn't it?"

By mid-speech he looked as if he was going to come up out of his chair. By the time I was finished, he leaned back and sighed with weary resignation. I fought off the empathy that a man has when he knows exactly how the other guy feels and can't do a goddamned thing to help.

"All right, Hopper. I'll be the Burger King and you can have it your way. For now. But when this is all over—"

"I'm hoping that I will have made a friend for life, Ketchum."

"Horseshit. How's that go? With friends like you, who needs enemies? What's next?"

Now, any stray woman who might have been in that room would have thought the Chief was still mad and suspicious. Women get real literal about the way men speak to one another. But I knew that "horseshit" was just a way of acknowledging that I was right about all of it, including the lifetime friendship, and that he wasn't about to deal with it just then. He wanted his role back and he wanted to be part of the plan.

"Tighten the surveillance on Arnie and Mimi," I said then. "Help me find or create an event that includes the gang of four. I need Gaiters, Casey, Lavelle, and McCain at the same social occasion at the same time."

"To do what?"

"I'm going to get them to make a buy from my operative."

"That's entrapment."

"Not the way I'm going to do it."

"And I suppose you're not going to tell me how you're going to do it."

"Let's just call it Western justice."

"All right. Let me see what I can do about the gang of four." Ketchum was quiet for a moment. "You know, I'm a little surprised that Arnie hasn't been to see Mimi."

"I suspect he thinks you're going to pop him if he shows up. I want to know how he got by the tail you put on Brock. Arnie's not that clever, you know."

"My guy said he was chasing Arnie all over the county on the old bike when Arnie must have figured it out and took off through the trees. It's pretty hard to push a Pontiac through the same holes as a Harley. We couldn't have done any better with only one tail. Sometimes life's a shit sandwich."

The final jolt was the opportunity knocking at my door. This time it was Cochise. He and Doug nodded to each other even before I made the introductions. Doug looked like he was disposed to stay and Cochise looked like his lips were sealed until Doug skedaddled. I ushered Ketchum out diplomatically. When I turned around, Little Brother was chewing on a toothpick and looking smug.

"I thought you had a full-time babysitting job with the chemist," I said.

"It's handled. Not to worry."

I shrugged. I had enough to worry about.

"Well, I did good on my first assignment, Hopper. Do I get to finish the job or not?"

"Yes. As a matter of fact you do. The first part of finishing the job is to do a little disposition planning."

"Who are we disposing of?"

"The little kingpins. I need two things from you. Any ideas on how to get them in the same room with you at the same time for some innocuous reason? Then I need the name of exactly the right drug."

"Right drug for what?"

"For a disability. We're not going to take them out, we're just going to take them out of commission."

"Temporarily? Shit, what good does that do?"

"Not temporarily, permanently."

"You want a drug that's going to cripple them but not kill them? Hopper, you been into the Black Jack too heavy. Wounded tigers are dangerous critters. If you're going to wound 'em, you might as well finish 'em off."

"You're not listening very well today. I didn't say cripple, I said disable."

"You mean like inducing a stroke or a coma?"

"Something like that. But the only problem with stroke and coma is that you can recover. I remember something about an episode in California. Just can't dredge up enough details. I think a heroin-like narcotic analgesic might have been involved."

Little Brother frowned. I didn't know whether he was reviewing the drug manual he keeps in his head or whether he was bothered by the concept. Suddenly his face cleared and he whistled through his teeth.

"Jesus, Hopper, that's a beauty."

"What?"

"I gotta drug that will put those guys in the land of the living dead. Permanent neurological impairment. Big-time chronic agony. And I thought that I was the diabolical member of this cadre. You're way ahead of me. You know, it would be a lot kinder to just kill them, but I gotta admit, this is a pretty righteous form of retaliation you're talking about here."

"What's the drug and what's the disability?"

"MPTP. Ecstasy lost. Works like the herbicide paraquat. It's what happens when you make a mistake whipping up a batch of MPPP, a reverse ester of meperidine. The chemists call it a bad synthesis. The brew gets too hot—too acidic. Causes severe Parkinson's very quickly, even in moderate doses. It selectively destroys cells in the substantia nigra and the straitum. Those are the dopamine brain cells. Dopamine's a neurochemical transmitter without which control of movement is lost. Among other things, it produces what's known as Bradykinesia—a poverty of all movements. Once taken, there's enough of a delayed reaction to make it almost foolproof, since the only known antidote is useless unless administered immediately."

Something about the cool efficiency of his description pulled me up short. That and the memory of the few cases of Parkinson's that I've ever seen. There is rigidity and tremor. Limbs don't move well and even the head may shake involuntarily. Balance is disturbed and walking is often interrupted by stops to get it all back together. Secondary symptoms include depression, sleep disorders, constipation, sexual dysfunction, dizziness—even senility, which may grow to resemble Alzheimer's. When coordination of the mouth and tongue goes, clarity of speech goes with it. Legible writing is unlikely. And then there's the drooling. The living dead, Cochise had said.

I am suspicious of all actions that are motivated by the

human desire to hurt. These were bad guys, pure and simple. For some people that would have made the decision easy, but I wanted to be certain that the plan was not built on one angry man's sadistic impulses—namely mine. That would mean the plan failed the criterion of ethical soundness. I couldn't afford to be that self-indulgent.

I looked at Little Brother as if for a clue and he was staring at my face. Or was he reading my mind?

"It will get pretty ugly, Hopper. Prepare yourself for that."

"The only other option is to turn it over to the DEA now and let the Chief get the credit. My confidence level isn't very high on that one. Some of them will walk. I want them all."

"So let's do it. Get off your moral high horse. You asked for the right drug and I gave it to you. I'm not going into this caper without someone who's absolutely committed. I understand that you don't think of yourself as a guy who runs around turning people into zombies, but you're forgetting something, Hopper. You're forgetting how many people *they* turned into zombies while they were laughing all the way to the bank and building their big houses and getting turned on by their chickenshit power. They've been dealing in human lives, Hopper, and I'm not going to weep when the parasites get theirs. So I've got the drug solved and I can even get them in the same ballroom in the Richmond Country Club on Sunday night, but I'm not going to lift a finger until you tell me that you're over your tender little humanistic episode."

Little Brother usually isn't given to long speeches and blazing eyes. Sometimes I forget he's half Italian. He was hot about this one. He was also right. I guessed that there was still a part of me, though, that wished that "Western justice" didn't seem quite so close to guerrilla warfare and terrorism.

30

It was a strange time in Richmond. Shelley Stone, the Chamber of Commerce lady, had scheduled a community event for Sunday evening at the country club. Larry Covington had gotten his invitation verbally from a local attorney he'd met in Ethridges while being the degenerate yup. I didn't ask him how much bar coke the invite had cost him.

The event was to be the kickoff for a new promotional campaign for the city. I suspected that McCain would just as soon not have to deal with it. Shelley Stone was probably under some pressure about canceling the dinner out of respect for ex-Chief Brock's recent demise, but the flowers were ordered and the speaker was arranged. Poor

Shelley had no way of knowing what other pressures the city fathers were now under.

It gave me one day to get the drug made and delivered from Cabo. It could be obtained easily and most reliably through an old expatriate friend. Dave used to be in the drug-manufacturing business here in the U.S. until things got too hot. He wasn't really an exploiter, just an experimental chemist run somewhat amok. He was an encyclopedia for custom drugs and could create effects to order given information on an individual's psyche, body chemistry, and physique. He now filled special orders from special friends on a cash-as-needed basis. I trusted Dave's pride in his scientific abilities. The last thing I needed was a slipup based on street impurities. I called the Baja.

Stryker answered personally on the first ring, which gave me some indication that he had been in "ready" mode since our last phone call.

"Well," he said. "The plan is in place, I trust."

"Very nearly. The operative and I have a little more planning to do in terms of the actual event, but it's going to happen one way or the other on the Sabbath. At the country club. Nice touch, don't you think?"

"Hmmph. Be more precise."

"I will need to be very precise in about thirty seconds because I have a prescription for you to discuss with Dave. But first I'll give you the broad outlines of the drama as it's played out so far."

"Fine. Try to keep it brief. Maggie has consented to dine with me this evening and Lucia is making mole con pavo."

At times like these, I always suspect that Stryker reads some of the anxiety in my voice. It is then, while what I have on my mind is tremendously important to me, that he's most likely to convey some message that is not necessarily the most significant thing on *his* mind. It is a left-handed way of telling me that I'm going to make it through the current problem just as well as I've made it through the others. There was something about being told that mole con pavo and an evening with his lady were important too that was remarkably reassuring. It put the whole friggin' mess in perspective. What I was about to do was dirty and dangerous, but he wasn't overly concerned about it and I shouldn't be either.

"It becomes clearer that the DEA agent was about to stumble into the same rat's nest that Doug suspected. I don't know who did him, but I suspect that the locals fingered him and their K.C. partners did the number."

"And the girl?"

"Odds are it was Brock. I have two hypotheses. My first is that Gaiters got loose-lipped one night, told her too much, and then told Brock to take care of it before she told anyone else. My second is that Arnie started to ask for a bigger piece of the pie because the DEA might turn the heat up and his risk was greater. Murdering Slew was a way of saying 'no way.' "

"And Brock's death?"

"Almost certainly Arnie. Straight vendetta on behalf of the dead girlfriend and the fractured half-sister, although it was too damned late if you ask me. Revenge with an undertone of telling Casey and the other big boys that Arnie has some firepower of his own."

"Plausible. Who runs this show?"

"Casey, I think. Gaiters, from all accounts, is too venal and stupid for the kind of negotiating they've apparently done with the K.C. boys. McCain makes everything all right politically but probably couldn't have capitalized this gig, and Lavelle is just the guardian against accidental legal exposure."

"Why haven't they gotten rid of Ketchum? He's an obtrusive, intelligent threat to them."

"I honestly don't know, although Casey is probably

smart enough to see Doug for what he is—a bulldog. Unless they fully intend to kill him at some point, they know they can't dismiss him because he'll go squawking all the way to Washington with this much evidence."

"And the prescription?"

"We're going to feed them some MPTP, which works a little like the herbicide paraquat, and wait a few hours for Parkinson's disease to develop. With the lab gone and the Richmond players on their way to chronic-care facilities, K.C. will be forced to go elsewhere."

"Hmmph. Seems like extraordinary means when you have a good beginning on a case for the DEA. Might you have been seduced into their own patterns of overkill? Are you killing flies with a meat cleaver, bullfrog?"

"You said there were other kinds of death besides the final rattle. I took it to heart."

"I understand. What are the short-term moves?"

"Send someone to Dave and tell him what we need. The chemical formula is one methyl, four phenyl, one, two, three, six tetrahydropyridine. I'll fax that formula and a diagram to you, although he probably won't need it. With the diagram will be physical descriptions of the targets so he can design the dose properly. He may need to see the slight deviation in the molecule. He might need someone to make a jet-assisted shopping trip to a chemical store stateside. I suspect Sergio can arrange that. Then Dave hands off to Sergio. Sergio packs the diplomatic pouch, waves his wand, and I'll pick it up myself."

"Simple enough. Anything else?"

"Yeah, have Lucia put any leftover mole con pavo in the freezer, and kiss Maggie for me."

"Consider it done. Godspeed, bullfrog."

31

When things get down to the short hairs, everybody winds themselves up to full tension, each betting on his own game plan to prevail. According to my gut, B. F. Hopper and the Richmond boys were now at the ten-dollar window. Was the gang of four meeting somewhere in town plotting to change the odds? Were stress cracks in the alliance starting to create a handicap? It was likely that Brock's death had left no line officer to make the biker chieftain run his mules. No drug traffic out. No yuppie car traffic in. And where was that sad, vengeful, and violent biker chieftain, anyway?

When you crave action, nothing seems to happen. It's all part of the silent stalking. I sat in the hotel room after

I hung up with Stryker and I reviewed the situation. Then I re-reviewed it. I had nothing to do until the pouch drop on Saturday. I wanted to be movin' and jivin', and I was sittin' and stewin' instead. Time does not fly when you are not having fun.

For the first time in a while, I had a chance to think about Mimi. Doug's hired hand had called me on Thursday to tell me that she was home and he would be on the job until the Chief called him off. I didn't ask if I could talk to her. I figured she would call when she was ready to forgive me for rearranging her life. I thought about her pulverized face and hoped like hell that it was going to heal in a way that would leave her able to cope after this drug war was over. Healing could happen with her face, but it was too late for it to happen with her life, since that had been caught up in a harshness of reality from the day she was born.

Slew and Mimi were a counterpoint in innocence for me. Slew had been born with the potential to be victimized. She never really understood it and died from a lack of the protection that such innocents require. Mimi had also been born with the potential to be victimized. She understood every painful detail of her circumstances and stayed alive by refusing protection from those who were weaker than she and by stubbornly refusing her innocence.

And Arnie, far from being the vicious joker in the pack, was instead a foil for the tragedy. Arnie's whereabouts were beginning to bug me. I didn't think I had nearly enough of what he knew. I took my restlessness to Geek's. It was a Friday night but the bar was nearly empty. A few guys in colors were sitting around with the biker equivalent of the typing pool. Female biker groupies without a steady old man. When I got to the door, Geek was wiping glasses and looking somber. I looked at the weariness in his shoulders and the set of his frown. For a split second he seemed to bear the same burden that Stryker bore, of knowing too much, and of being required to watch the next generation live through the same fuck-ups that had plagued his own.

I waited at the door until I could catch his eye. I got it finally. He eyes weren't hostile this time. Just wary. I approached the bar slowly, not pushing it. He tolerated me like a wounded animal tolerates a vet with a scalpel. I made it onto the bar stool without a challenge.

"Gimme a beer, Geek."

He didn't acknowledge me except to remember that the last time I was here I'd ordered a Stroh's. He fetched one for me now, pounding it on the bar in front of me before he continued wiping the glasses. I spoke to his back because there was no one else at the bar and I didn't need to see his face.

"I need to find Arnie."

"Sounds like a personal problem to me, man."

He spoke softly but without menace. It was as if there was something stored up inside that he really needed to tell me. I kept my voice somewhere between confidential and casual.

"Geek, there's not a lot I can tell you about what's coming down. Shit, you've probably known about most of it forever."

I paused to see if the heat-seeking missile was going to reach the target. He finally turned around and stared. It was enough encouragement for me. I continued.

"I don't even know if you give a shit about Arnie's health and happiness, but we both know that his ass is in a crack right now with Brock out of the picture. He's got no buffer and he's number one on the hit list."

"So what do you want with him, Farber? You're just out-of-town heat, as far I can see."

"I want to talk to him, Geek. I want to get to him before Gaiters and McCain and Lavelle have him for lunch."

The stare got colder and hotter at the same time.

167

"So why don't you just call him on the phone? Drop by the house for a little visit. Maybe he'll brew up a spot of tea. I'm sure he wants to talk to you, too. Especially since you've come here to save his ass. Give me a break."

"The cops tell me they see him around town but they don't see him go home. He doesn't answer his phone. He hasn't been there since Brock was found facedown in the ditch with his throat slit. Tell me where to call him, Geek. Where to visit him."

There wasn't much sound in the bar beyond the juke rolling out the Rolling Stones' "Honky Tonk Woman." The bikers were concentrating on their beers and the biker groupies.

Geek looked at me as though I were a recalcitrant child.

"Look," he said. "If Arnie was in trouble, where do you think he would be? Somewhere I didn't know about? Not on your life, bud. I pulled that motherfucker out of a hole in Cambodia just before the big ones went off and I ain't taken my eyes off him since. You wanna see Arnie right now, you see me."

I paused again because I was damned if Geek wasn't starting to make sense to me as the paterfamilias of this crew.

"So I'm asking, Geek."

He didn't say anything. I moved in.

"Or is it Sergeant Geek? Or perhaps even Lieutenant Geek. I think the fog is beginning to clear a bit."

The bikers stayed quiet. And suddenly Geek threw back his head and laughed from the depth of some secret history in which he hadn't always been the quintessential Hell's Angel. It was a sardonic laugh.

"Christ, he's in my apartment over the bar. You don't need a key. Just go on up there and do whatever you're gonna do. I got no stomach for him right now, but the man wasn't like this when ..."

The laughter was gone and the voice trailed off. I wondered who or what Arnie had been to Geek when...

I followed Geek's shrug toward the door. There was an outside stairway up to a small porch. I walked up the rickety stairs and knocked on the cheap hollow-core door.

To this day, I'll never know whether it was Arnie or his ghost who answered, but the man appeared to have lost ten pounds and the circles under his eyes were a deep purple-gray and half the size of his cheeks.

He took me in passively and there was less panic in his face than anxious resignation.

"Well, Arnie, it's time for us to talk. Even Geek thinks so. Let's find someplace a little more comfortable than the doorway, what do you say?"

Arnie backed up into what must have been Geek's living room, although it was indistinguishable from most day rooms in nursing homes for the criminally insane.

Arnie's eyes, which looked remarkably like Mimi's, were doing a crazy dance as I backed him up to a chair into which he collapsed like a geriatric helium balloon.

"Hey, man. This isn't what you think. It wasn't me, man. I didn't blow up that place and I didn't kill nobody. Not nobody."

His eyes watered and I couldn't tell whether he was waiting for me to hammer him or whether he was overdrawn on the bar-coke account.

"I'm about done cutting you slack. Seems to me that outside of Brock, who's in a satin-lined box being adored by family and friends, you're the only guy in these parts who may know more than me about this scam."

He was sitting in the chair and I was standing over him like Attila or Godzilla or some other monster of the silver screen.

"I didn't do nuthin, man. I didn't off Brock."

"Cut the crap, Arnie. I don't care if you did. You killed

Slew just as sure as if you'd put a gun to her head. You almost killed Mimi. And then, because your feeble conscience was bothering you, you killed Brock. It was your attempt to settle up."

I saw his eyelids tighten. I saw his lips move, and he came up out of the chair like a wounded dog. I had been waiting for this. No real surprise. But there was something about the way his fist was clenched and the rage in his eyes that primed all of my muscles for defense.

The reason that so many punches in the movies are done in slow motion is that slow motion is the way it really feels. So in a split second that felt like a century, I saw the knife come off his hip, the blade snap open and start toward my gut. My left arm came up instinctively to parry the blade hand while my right drove his belly button into his spine. When he doubled over, my knee came up into his chin to crack his jaw and give him a couple of teeth loose enough to spit in his soup. Arnie sat down in the chair looking dazed.

"Don't try it again, Arnie. I came here to talk and if you don't want to do that, I'm going to deliver you to Ketchum in a basket. I have a little ledger book I found in your library that I think they'd be interested in."

Arnie leaned forward and closed his eyes against my interrogation.

"Arnie, I can help you or I can deliver you. Start thinking about whose tender mercies you trust. Your choices are me and Doug or Gaiters and McCain. I don't really care who ends up taking you out."

"I don't trust anyone, Hopper. 'Cept maybe Geek, and look at what he just did to me."

"Look, tough guy, if I dump you on Ketchum's doorstep, he'll squeeze the information out of you. And don't count on your so-called buddies at City Hall to get you off the hook. You flipped them a big bird when you took out Brock. What I would rather do is give you a chance at life in exile in exchange for an explanation of how the Richmond-K.C. scam works."

"Why should I help you?"

"Because I can get you out of this alive." I grabbed a kitchen chair and planted it in front of the single exit from Geek's one-room habitat. "Besides, you're not going anywhere until I let you."

Arnie looked caged by the flimsy chair. "So save me, Hopper. Maybe it'll get you a bronze star."

"We're going to have this conversation and then you're going to get out of town. I'll cover for you until you have a decent head start. I have to make the offer now because I suspect that there are things you're going to tell me that might make me change my mind. The deal is real, Arnie. I'm real. You have to trust me. But I want it all or I'll burn you. You are quickly running out of options."

Arnie rose slowly from the chair without any sign of a threat. He looked young and wounded in the eyes, old and battered in the face, and embittered in his stance.

"Where do you want me to start?"

"How did you get involved with Luther Brock? Mimi says that Brock's guys used to hassle anyone in colors for nothing at all. Suddenly that all stopped. What was the very first deal, Arnie?"

His right shoulder rose and fell in an involuntary defensive gesture. He began to pace.

"I got popped on a small charge. Public drunkenness, I think it was. When I got out of jail, Brock called and wanted to talk to me about 'insurance.' So I talked to him."

"Yeah, what kind of policy did he offer you?"

"Said he had some friends in high places who could take the heat off my guys and make us some money at the same time. Said he liked the idea of using my troops. Liked their discipline, their loyalty, and their balls. Said it was just the right kind of job for us."

"What kind of job?"

171

Arnie snorted. "Deliveries. Kind of like Domino's Pizza. We'd run drugs to the K.C. families and come back with cash and hot cars to order."

"And what kind of pizza were you delivering?"

"At first it was just the usual. Mexican garbage mostly. Ganja, purple haze, some copilots, and some soaps. Then we got some pretty large quantities of high-quality toot and heroin. Kinda upped the stakes. We started taking requests, and things really began to get complex. Better lab stuff. More meth, crank, lotsa crack. A little angel dust."

"Spell it out for me, Arnie. I want details. Who did you get the drugs from here? Who did they go to in K.C.? Who got the cars and the cash when you got back?"

Arnie's brow knitted in resistance. "I thought you said you knew almost as much as me, Hopper. You ain't got shit."

"Okay, I'll tell you what I know and you nod your head when I'm right and fill in the blanks. Kind of like Twenty Questions. The vanilla drugs came up from Mexico through the usual channels, and the outbuilding on Casey's farm was just the dilution and distribution center for a while. Then the clients started asking for more and the stakes were bigger. Stuff started coming in from Florida and directly from Central and South America."

Arnie nodded and looked at the floor.

"Then Casey, the businessman who knows all about margins, decided that cutting out the importers and the jobbers would boost his profits. How'm I doing?"

"Not bad. About six months into it, Brock told me to find a chemist. Only when I got Brock the cook, I didn't know Casey managed the bankroll."

"When did you find out?"

"The chemist was a biker from Georgia who's cousin to one of my guys. He became my pipeline. Brock was supposed to keep us in the dark and protect the hotshots, but he got a little careless with his mouth when he was drunk. Started acting like he didn't really care what I knew."

"Why is that?"

"Guess he figured he could send me up whenever he wanted. Even then I didn't know Gaiters and Lavelle had anything to do with it."

"When did that come out?"

"We used to have a guy involved who got greedy and started to deal on his own. He dealt some shit to a young kid who sold it to a high-school kid who got caught by one of Ketchum's guys. Lavelle didn't even—"

"You can move on, Arnie. I know that story."

"So I figured those guys had to be a part of it somehow. McCain wasn't too tough to figure either. He's got a stupid son who runs a used-car lot. We'd make the trade in K.C. and run the cars back to an empty warehouse just south of here in Henrietta. An empty building that's part of a big over-the-road trucking operation there. It was a chop shop. Brock kept some of the cops and a couple of my guys busy there partin' 'em out or changin' numbers, colors, and options around for export. Some of 'em turned up on McCain's used-car lot. I don't know how much Joe McCain knows, probably not much. I'm sure his old man provided the cars and fed him some story. The Audi that the Mayor drives is one I picked up personally in K.C. about a year ago."

"So how does the money get cut?"

"I'm not sure, man. I think Casey takes his off the top. Brock gets a piece for running the street organization and for providing police protection. His boys and mine have been known to run cars to a front in Houston where they get shipped offshore I guess."

"Why the ledger book, Arnie? If you were just the mule, what did you care what went where? And how did you know?"

"Well, there for a while, Brock was real happy about the

job we were doing for him. Shit, we thought it was easy money. But he kinda rewarded me with this new job, y'know. I got a little more of the action for helping him keep track of the traffic."

Arnie sat back down in the chair. His posture had changed. It was as if the opportunity to tell the story had stirred up something inside him that motivated him to make sense out of the whole mess. That suited me just fine. I'd started with a reluctant informant and now I had what Stryker would call a "street raconteur."

"What about Lavelle and Gaiters?"

"I don't think Lavelle and Gaiters were in until Casey had to figure out a way to get rid of the charges against that high-school kid. I suspect that when Brock was the Chief, those three did all kinds of illegal shit. I don't think Lavelle is in for much, but it brings him more bucks than he's going to make being a podunk prosecutor. Gaiters is another story."

Arnie's posture changed again. He started to shrink into the crummy chair because we were approaching the point in the story at which he stopped being a cynical biker who just wanted to score some bread and some excitement. We were approaching the point where he started to become a piece of dog shit even by his own antisocial standards.

"So what's the news on Gaiters?"

"I don't know much about Gaiters. He gives light sentences or probation when Casey tells him to. Or maybe it's Brock who calls the shots. Hell, I don't know."

"Looks like we have to go back to Twenty Questions, Arnie. I'll tell you about Gaiters. You tell me when I'm right."

Arnie looked up at me as if he'd do just about anything to get out of the room, but I checked his large muscles for movement and saw no signs that he was on his way out of the chair again.

"Gaiters is the weirdo in the crew. You knew he was shtupping your sister in lieu of bail for a long time, didn't you?"

"She isn't my sister."

"Oh, shut up, Arnie, you're not helping yourself by bringing up irrelevant details. She's your half-sister. Sister, half-sister, who cares? All I care about is figuring out how Slew got pulled into the loop. Mimi thinks Slew was a bargaining chip during a tough negotiation. Was she?"

"Mimi thinks that? She told you that?"

He looked like a kid whose mother had just caught him reading his father's porn. He looked less like a tough-assed biker and more like a ten-year-old who had started lying early to keep himself out of trouble. Sometimes even lying to himself.

"Yeah, Arnie. She thinks that. So do I. If you have another explanation, I'll listen to it. If you don't, so what? What do I care if you can't live with yourself? You made that bed. I need to hear the information, Arnie, not your confession to being a jerk."

He hung his head. I don't think it was guilt. Guilt is when you feel bad about something you did. I think this was shame, which is when you feel bad about who you are. This was Arnie the whore's kid. Arnie the poor kid. Arnie the bully. Arnie the high-school dropout. Arnie the vet who survived when his buddies didn't, sometimes at their expense. Arnie who stood accused by his own half-sister of committing psychological incest and pimping his "property" until she died from it.

I watched the desperation play across his face, and I knew I wouldn't need to mete out much more punishment because he was doing it to himself in a way that no one else could. The punishment was internal, exquisitely masochistic, and it would be ongoing for as long as he lived. I waited for the rationalizations that must inevitably come. I wasn't interested in them per se, but I was curious to see how he had been writing them off for so long. I wanted to listen carefully to cull out any facts that might help me in the next forty-eight hours.

"I knew about Mimi," Arnie said. "Sure, I knew. She did the crime and she didn't want to do the time. That's all it was, man. It was her choice. I didn't tell her to be a hooker. I didn't tell her to get it on with old-man Gaiters. That's on her."

"I didn't ask you about Mimi. I asked you about Slew."

"Aw, man. Slew's a different story. For the first six months, I didn't even know what was going on. Gaiters told her not to tell me because I'd get mad and then he'd have to hurt me and all the money would stop. Slew wasn't smart, but she wasn't stupid either. So she did what he told her. She never said a word."

"How did you find out?"

"Brock."

"How?"

"He was paying me off one day and he laid an extra five hundred dollars on me as a 'bonus.' I ain't used to nobody laying money on me that I haven't delivered something on. I asked him what the bonus was for. He screwed up that slimy face of his and told me. Then he laughed. Told me I was smarter than I looked. Told me Slew was even better than Mimi because she did whatever Gaiters wanted with no back-talk. Said Gaiters really loved it because Mimi just went through the motions but Slew really got into it. I wanted to cut his fucking dick off, man. His and Gaiters's both."

He wasn't looking at me. I don't think he even knew I was still there. He was talkin' to himself. Trying to explain it.

"Then I talked to Slew and she cried and told me not to beat on her. Shit, I never beat on her in my life. She'd do something really stupid and I'd just let it go by because I knew the way she was and she couldn't help it none."

"How long ago did you find out, Arnie?"

He looked clear away from me then.

"What difference does that make, Hopper?"

"How *long* ago, dammit?"

"A year. A little over maybe."

"You had some leverage, Arnie. You knew a lot. They couldn't replace you easily. Why'd you let it go on? Why didn't you buy her out of it?"

"Because of her. She didn't want me to."

"Arnie, if you are about to give me some chickenshit story about Slew being into Gaiters, I'm going to mop up Geek's filthy floor with you, crumple you up like an old cigarette pack, and toss you into the dumpster with the rest of the garbage. What the hell do you mean she didn't want you to?"

"She was sure that they'd find a way to cut me out of the deal if she didn't keep Gaiters's kinky little appetites fed. He told her that over and over. Brock told me the same thing. She liked the money. She said she didn't mind. See, Hopper, Gaiters had it wrong. Even though she did all the bizarre stuff he wanted as easily as the churchies do the missionary number, it was Slew who just went through the motions. Sex wasn't anything to her except something she'd learned to do to please men. Hangin' around with the bikers, she learned a lot and practiced it often."

"She liked the money? Didn't mind? Slew wasn't into money, Arnie. She was into you. You liked the money and so she said she didn't mind. I'm in no mood for this fairy tale, man. Your sister was right. You sold her to Gaiters to keep the bucks coming through the pipeline."

Some black rage was overcoming me and I didn't know why. It wasn't as if I hadn't speculated on exactly what Arnie was confirming. God knows, I'd heard worse. But hearing it offended some part of me that didn't believe that she didn't mind. I was in the process of what Stryker calls "going polar." The needle was pegged. I was at a crazy, hostile point and I didn't want to hear another word from him. I couldn't be in the conversation anymore. There was no dialogue possible. Just the monologue that pressed my tongue into action. I wanted to hurt him.

"So where'd you learn to pimp, Arnie? Helping your mom when you were a kid? Did you get a cut of her action, too?"

I'd already gotten out of the chair because in my world there's only one thing worse that you can accuse a man of and I didn't expect that Arnie would stop to notice that I was bigger than he was. He'd have to come after me on male principle. In good martial arts form, I wasn't watching his face, I was watching his overall intention.

I heard Stryker-in-my-head, only this time I also saw him. Stryker in video instead of just audio is a sure sign that I am hurtling toward some edge where he has to serve as the emergency brake. "All hatred starts as compassion that is frustrated by circumstance," I heard him say in that hypnotic bass voice with the omnipresent stern features, motionless and controlling.

My head snapped up to take a closer look at Arnie, who was not moving. He looked like a corpse. I felt like an exterminator. I had exterminated the last shred of self-respect that he had saved by painstakingly preserving that early secret, which I had hit upon in a fit of righteous sarcasm.

The corpse spoke. Or was it the ghost?

"Did my sister tell you that, Hopper? She wasn't supposed to know." The biker chieftain's voice was wispy. I'd been right the first time. It was shame, not guilt.

I would come to feel the compassion frustrated by circumstance but only much later. Just then I needed to attend to my initial purpose, which was information. I didn't look at him. I just rapped out the final question.

"Who killed her, Arnie?"

"Brock, I guess. I didn't stop to ask him before I slit his throat."

That was as much as I needed. I was content to let Brock's murderer get away. In fact, the sooner he was out of my sight, the better for both of us.

"I'll let that one go, Arnie. Just know that I know. One last question. What makes Gaiters so weird? What's his number?"

Arnie stood up. He looked like an inmate in *One Flew Over the Cuckoo's Nest*. Beaten to death while he still lived and breathed.

"Gaiters was always mean. Liked being a judge because it gave him power over other people's lives. Now it's the crack. But he didn't start using it heavily until he got into this scam with Casey. He's fucked up a lot of the time."

"Who else?"

"McCain. A little less, maybe. Casey not at all. Lavelle on the weekends. Hopper?"

"Yeah?"

"You're really going to let me up? I can get the hell out of here?"

"Yeah."

"You like my sister, don't you?"

"I like her a lot. Why?"

"Tell her good-bye for me? Tell her I ... "

"Don't stop at your house, Arnie. Don't take the hard-tail. Borrow a bike from someone you trust. Go and don't come back. I'll handle it with Ketchum. And I'll talk to Mimi."

We stared at each other like strangers who know each other much better than they have a right to. I put the chair back at the kitchen table and left without saying goodbye.

On the way out, I stuck my head in the bar.

"Arnie's got his marching orders, Geek. Help him go."

No further explanation was necessary. The surly biker bartender saluted and I left to get the kind of sleep that is intruded upon by other people's nightmares.

32

By eight on Saturday morning, I was wiring the nerves and muscles that always get me through the final act. Stryker didn't call until ten, by which time I was fine-tuned and in concert mode. Arnie's story made it easy for me to get on with it. If Arnie did what I told him and got out of town, I would square it with Doug. If he hadn't, then he was on his own and my debt was paid in full.

The Professor was terse. He had spoken with Dave and had reassured him that the drugs were for me and the operation was protected against being traced. The Professor seemed a little annoyed at being asked. Dave and I had always had an understanding, but he was still a little scared of Stryker, probably rightly so.

"What's the pouch itinerary?" I asked him.

"Sergio has arranged for a private Lear with diplomatic status from the States to drop by the strip at the Hotel Cabo San Lucas just north of here on Chileno Bay. It will clear customs without fuss in Houston, where they're used to such things. From there it's nonstop to Lexington, Missouri. There are no constraints to your pickup. With about four and a half hours in the air and not more than an hour in Houston, you should plan to meet them no later than nine tonight. Be at the airport and the courier will find you."

"He won't have any trouble finding me. I'll be in the car on the taxiway near the center of the strip. He's got thirty-three hundred feet on Runway Twenty-two. Hope he has short-field capability and some guts. . . . A Lear, huh? Well, I guess I won't have any trouble recognizing him. Don't see many Lears in Lexington, Missoura."

"They've checked out the field and can manage it. Lawless is using his own man. It's simple. Really, Hopper. Sometimes you sound like a bad novel. What's happened to you in Missouri?"

"I've become very tired and even more cynical—if that's possible. But that can wait until I get to Cabo. Your deck."

"Then wrap it up and get your ass back to the command post."

"Yes, sir! I'm doing my best. No sign of the DEA yet. Just as well. They might frown on our technique."

"You can thank Lawless for their absence."

"That will be the day."

This time neither one of us said good-bye.

The Elms was beginning to wear on me. I called Cochise and he was surly, too.

"So, Little Brother, what is Larry the yup doing in Excelsior Springs this fine Saturday?"

"Ironin' my party clothes, babe, and keepin' an eye on

things. Cementing relationships. Waiting for my Boy Scout partner in this gig to make a decision to pull his head out of the sand and get moving."

I cocked an eyebrow when I heard "Boy Scout partner." He was really antsy. In other circumstances, the man would not have dared, but in muggy Missouri at this very moment, there was no point in not daring. He wanted to get it off the dime in a bad way.

"Where's the chemist?" I asked him. "I need to talk to him. We also have a brief side trip to make to an airport by the mighty Mo."

"What do you mean 'we'?"

"Don't give me any white-man shit, fool. I need to talk to the chemist and you need to get your ass to the Lexington airport with me by nine this evening. It is now noon. Now, are you going to get it done?"

"You know, Hopper, you were grumpy when you invited me to this party and you're still grumpy. Where do you want to talk to the chemist?"

"Well, I assume he's not presentable enough for here and I don't want to parade him around Richmond. Meet me in the parking lot of the Ray County Historical Museum. What time can you get him there?"

"He's twenty minutes away and he doesn't have a lot of other appointments. Jesus, Hopper. I'll be there in thirty minutes, by which time I hope you manage to get the cayenne pepper out of your jock."

"All right, Cochise. Button it up. There's news you don't have. I haven't really turned into a flaming asshole. I just sound that way."

"Yeah. Easy for you to say. You don't have to listen to yourself. You're being such a jerk, I'm beginning to miss my Voc Rehab patients."

"Be patient. The end is near, as they say."

"As who says?"

"I'll see you at the museum."

There were only two pieces of information that I needed from the chef. The first was who handed him his cash. The second was what he had been cranking out of his Cuisinart lately.

Sometimes, when I don't want to do something, I will arrange to do it when I don't have enough time to spend more than a few minutes at the task. I dialed Mimi's number hoping to get Doug's Doberman, from whom I would get a nice report about her welfare. No such luck.

"Hello."

She sounded as though the fat lip was on the mend. That meant we could communicate, and that was of even more concern than having to worry about her pain. She might say something that I didn't want to hear.

"Mimi. It's Hopper. I wanted to ... Shit, I don't know what I wanted to do. Just hear your voice, I guess. I knew you were doing all right. I got that from your trusty guard. And Doug. Are they telling me the truth?"

"Richmond's finest? Of course, they're telling the truth. But never mind that, Hopper. Have you seen Arnie? I can't find him. No one can find him."

There was a mournful tone in her voice and I thought about all that Mimi had lost in the last two weeks. Her surrogate sister. Her relative security under the blows of Brock's goons. Her tormenter. Her half-brother. Her role.

I wasn't sure what I was going to say, but my mouth opened anyway and I waited to hear what my unconscious thought I ought to say to this tender-hearted, redheaded roundheels.

"Yeah, I've seen Arnie. With any luck, he's out of the state. He told me to say good-bye. And to apologize. I need to talk with you, but I can't get there until Monday. I know it's not good enough, but it's the best I can do right now."

I felt like a public defender with too many cases who

didn't even have the time to meet an accused before it was time to appear in court. I felt as though I was treating her the way everyone else had treated her all her life. As an anonymous, small-town bad girl who couldn't even command the respect her scummy brother got from his motorcycle club or the sympathy her little almost-sister got for her touching innocence.

And then I heard her voice, strong and intelligent. It caved me in.

"I can wait until Monday, Hopper. What's happening here is just another soap opera and they don't run over the weekends. I've put my life on hold so many times, another two days won't matter. I mean that. I have a feeling that whatever you're doing is the right thing to do, and I don't have anything to base that on but my gut. So far, that's been good enough. Thanks for calling. And thanks for your help."

She hung up the phone and so did I. The whole exchange reminded me of a story that Stryker once told me about Maggie. Maggie is the quiet love of Stryker's life. Half secret and half protected by his unwillingness to admit to his own attachment. Few people in Cabo know what Maggie does for a living—few anywhere, for that matter. Most people just think she's wealthy and worldly. In fact, what Maggie does for a living is somewhat akin to Mimi's trade. Same story set in a different neighborhood. Global, gentried, mature jet-set johns. And the story Stryker told had to do with the night Maggie disclosed that fact and took him to bed without any intention of submitting a bill. I was cheeky and naive then.

"Sounds like a coup, Stryker. Sounds like a hell of a bargain." I nearly pounded him on the back in my hurry to encourage his hail-fellow-well-met-conquest-of-not-so-fair-courtesan.

Stryker just stared at me colder than liquid nitrogen.

"You understand nothing about the psychological costs of honesty, bullfrog. You understand nothing about grace. I don't care what she does or does not do. I care that she is the kind of woman who can tell the truth about herself to those she really cares for. Some women are born with that dignity and you will not understand it until you have lived a good deal more of your life."

When he told the tale, I was a chastised student who had managed to offend the sensei one more time. And now I was older and wiser and I could feel Maggie's dignity in Mimi as she expressed her trust and thanked me for my help even while she dismissed me as a protector.

I was due at the museum and I tucked the reminder away for later. The chemist was the last piece of homework before the final initiative.

33

I made it to the museum, once the county poor farm, five minutes late. I spotted the righteous look on Little Brother's face before I even got out of my car. The chemist was pretty much everything he'd said. A bearded dildo. Half bald with the kind of beard that was thin even when it was full grown. He looked like a drummer from the sixties named Ginger Baker but with less hair. I walked over to their car and climbed into the backseat behind what's-his-name.

"So, bro. Good to see you're still on the job," Cochise said to me.

Love him as I do, I was about to take Little Brother's neck and wring it till it snapped. I refused to respond to his greeting and gave the chemist the once-over. He looked nervous. I didn't know whether it was the sweat on his palms or his underarms that exuded the rancid odor.

"I understand you've been spending some time with my friend here," I said to him.

The chemist didn't show any facial expressions. He was waiting for me to do whatever I was going to do to him, but he didn't want to chat.

"You understand that we're going to bring this house of cards down and you have the unique opportunity of helping or having us rip your eyes out."

"What do you want to know, man?" he said. "I ain't got all day."

Cochise leaned over subtly and gave him a short punch to the left side of his ribs.

"You got all day. All night too, asshole. You sit here and answer the man's questions if and when he decides to ask them."

The chemist leaned back, passive and pissed. I continued calmly.

"The rewards for helping are the usual. We can help you cop a lesser plea or turn state's witness. The consequences to not helping are that we might decide to beat the piss out of you and leave you worse than dead or turn you over to the cops. For you that probably means a long run at the Bijou on a habitual rap."

"Jesus Christ, I already told this guy as much as I know. And how you gonna make this stick when you abducted me and held me against my will? What the hell makes you think you can get away with this?"

"And just what makes you think we can't? Look, you've probably heard that possession is nine-tenths of the law. Well, now. We possess you, don't we? Abducted? We have been reading our law books, haven't we? We'll wire it any way we need to wire it. I don't give a flying fuck about what happens to you in the process."

I wasn't very concerned. The guy was clearly an opportunist. I like practicality in criminals. It makes them easier to deal with.

He lit up a joint Cochise had given him and took a deep drag.

"So what do you want to know that I haven't already told him?" he asked. He glared at Little Brother, and I suspected that Cochise had taken some pleasure in being rough on this victim of circumstances.

"I want to know about your product and your money. What's your menu been, say for the last six months?"

"Well, I started out just cuttin' Miss Emma and a little nose candy and whippin' up a batch or two of blotters. But you know bikers. I put the stuff together to make a little speed for the boys, but apparently the bucks in crack was a lot better. So mostly I've been doing that and some crank. Then things got more professionally demanding and I was getting requests for Pop and Ecstasy in small quantities."

"Why small quantities?"

"Keep the price up. There's not much on the market here yet and we control it."

"Who makes those decisions?"

"Dunno. The boys in Kansas City, I guess."

"And who gave you orders?"

"They were all written out for me when I'd get to the lab."

I looked at Cochise and he nodded to let me know we had some examples in our kit bag.

"Handwritten?"

"No. Typed up. All nice and neat."

"How did you get paid?"

"Cash. No withholding. New bills. Once a week."

"And who handed you the cash?"

"They left it with the instructions at the lab."

"Who's 'they'?"

"I dunno, man. I never saw anyone except Brock. And Arnie a couple of times when he was making a pickup. But they never gave me no money. I assume it came from the banker, but you can't prove it by me."

"Did you ever talk to Brock about who the banker or any of the other players might be?"

"What the hell did I care as long as I was getting paid?"

He was fiddling with his fingernails and I just didn't buy his blessed ignorance.

"You know, scumbag, I just don't believe that. In fact, I've been talking to Arnie, and he says you fed the bikers whatever you knew. You brothers do that for one another. Now, maybe you don't have a lot of privileged information, but you have a hell of a lot more than you're giving me and I don't consider that very damned cooperative."

I was staring at him in my most persuasive way and he squirmed in the seat.

"So you want to try it again?"

"Brock told me some stuff when I started. He told me that the guys behind this gig were bigshots in town who could protect the operation from just about everybody. He said he still ran the police force from the outside and they had a guy who could keep everybody out of court if something went wrong."

"But you never saw any of these dudes and Brock didn't use any names."

"Well, no, but Arnie and I figured some of it out. I didn't care, man. I been in plenty a drug operation with crooked cops, but never with anyone really powerful like a judge or a politician or nothing. Sounded to me like Brock was doin' it right and I just figured more power to him."

Ah yes, I thought, more power to the reprobate. Doing it right. We finished the conversation with a few personal questions about the chemist's history. There is a strange hierarchy in the drug underground. When I asked him where he'd learned his chemistry, he mentioned the name of a guy in California with whom he'd worked as an "apprentice." Cochise whistled softly between his teeth and looked at me.

"Damn. He was the best, Hopper. The very best. They wasted him in that sting operation the feds pulled off last year."

The chemist piped up nostalgically. "Yeah, man, and when he died, a whole lot of techniques died with him. The guy was a fuckin' genius. I've spent the whole last year tryin' to make some of the fentanyl analogs he created. Can't seem to get a handle on it."

It reminded me that men will create benchmarks of excellence and heroes to go with them, no matter what the industry.

I told Little Brother to stash the chemist again and to contact me at the Elms at six, then I went off to ponder heroes.

34

It was only two P.M. and the day seemed to stretch endlessly before me. I got into the Thunderbird to do the kind of meditation you can only do behind the wheel of a fast-moving car. I was becoming increasingly concerned that we were going to succeed in wiping out a significant drug factory at the expense of creating an untenable situation for Ketchum. I cranked the radio over to 71 A.M. and picked up WHB, where Wes Cunningham was playing "All Oldies All the Time," and headed south to 24, where there were some great flat straight stretches.

The chemist wasn't as great a witness as I had hoped, but his ability to testify to Brock's involvement and the production of illegal substances on Casey's farm would establish enough probable cause to move the system. If I took out Gaiters, Ketchum would have another judge to work with on the arrests. If I took out McCain, the City Council would be inclined to support Ketchum out of their own anxiety and because there was no one around to tell them any different. That was all upside.

On the other hand, I'd let Arnie up and he'd clear out only after he'd warned the other mules. He would take with him the only evidence I had against Lavelle, but it was only hearsay, anyway. And if Casey could get a good enough lawyer to argue that he didn't know about the illegal activities that were going on in an out-of-the-way building that he no longer used, he might walk. Not to mention that Doug would be put in the unenviable position of knowing that the sudden disability of Gaiters and McCain could be laid at my doorstep. And Little Brother's. I'd protected him as well as I could with the lie about entrapping them into making a buy. When the results were finally in, he'd have no real protection except his willingness to bend the truth in the interest of our mutual cause.

I looked at the speedometer on the T-bird as I blew by crossings at Fire Prairie Creek, Levisy, and the weigh station. It was pegged hard at 120 + , just next to but considerably faster than the river. I guess it induces alpha waves for me. I don't even notice.

I could solve the drug problem in the city of Richmond, but I couldn't help Doug with the ethical bind I was about to introduce into his world.

The meditation got unproductive. I swung north on 13 through Lexington, made another pass by the airport we were to use later, and headed back to the Elms to sit it out. When it got to be six P.M., Little Brother called and we agreed to meet for dinner.

We were both in the same mood. I was in the mood for a mood swing. We ate a lot because it was a better way to deal with impatience than drinking too much bourbon before the airport run. It was a "yang" meal with thick Midwestern steaks cooked rare and bloody. Huge baked potatoes swimming in sour cream and butter, going off the cholesterol chart forever. Large, leafy salads soaking in oily blue-cheese dressing and full of homemade croutons. Fat half ears of corn. Salty. Buttery. Topped with pecan pie made the way my Aunt Pearl used to make it. For Cochise it brought back memories of East Coast roadhouses where lawyers, Mafia hoods, and construction workers ate peacefully side by side because they just wanted a good meal. For me it was just like being back at Emil-enes near the airport in Denver. Or at my mother's special Sunday suppers in Two Buttes, when the ranch hands would join us and the fish stories got more outrageous with each course. It was the kind of meal that you ordered because there were hard times behind you and harder times in front of you, and the comfort foods were going to be the only oasis available for a while.

Little Brother was pressing me about the plan. By the time we got to coffee, I'd told him everything I knew from Arnie and he filled me in on scattered bits of intelligence that he'd gotten from the chemist. By the time we got to dessert, he was asking confrontational questions.

"So what's it going to be, Hopper? You got me up here to demolish a lab and that's done. I got you a witness. I can turn him over and go home now, if that's the way you want to play it."

"Simmer down, sidekick. We're going to leave here and pick up a package at the airport. Then we have some planning to do."

"Pick up a package? Now, that sounds like real man's work. What the hell's in the package?"

I looked at him with a glint in my eye because I enjoy giving people what they want.

"It's a diplomatic pouch, which is just fancy wrapping

for the potion you ordered. Happy now? You get to take out the bad guys. We get to do the whole schtick. We don't even have to say howdy-do to the DEA folks. How does that grab you?"

Cochise forked up the last morsel of pecan pie and grinned at me.

"You trying to tell me I've been a pain in the butt on this one?"

"Something like that. And while we're on the subject, what's gotten stuck in your craw about this one, anyway? Except for the municipal conspiracy angle, this job isn't much different from the stuff you've been doing for years. Why the Italian passion, guy?"

Little Brother made a big deal out of calling the waitress to get cream for his coffee, and when she brought it, he made a big deal of getting it into the cup and stirring it well. I was rolling my eyes by the time he deigned to answer my question.

"I guess it's Vivian Casey. I guess I get by just fine as long as all the victims and all the perpetrators are adults who are old enough to know which way is up. She isn't."

He looked down at the table and I could almost see him reviewing all the screwed-up kids who are the by-product of the big-money drug game. And I saw a solution to my misgivings about Casey getting his. The thought of playing Little Brother's heartstrings to get the job done was not something I allowed to be more than a fleeting consideration. Like my compassion for Arnie, my manipulation of my soft-hearted, kick-ass partner was going to have to wait for another time.

"So have you seen her since she helped you make the lab?" I asked him.

"Once. I was making a sale at the Hideaway and she came in. I finished the transaction and she sidled up and asked me to buy her a Coke. Jesus."

"What did you talk about?"

"Well, I had to keep the cover, so we pastimed about how much shit we'd consumed since we last saw each other. I was lying. I don't think she was. I also think she's scared as hell that she made a mistake by telling me. The only thing she said of any importance was that she was almost glad the lab was gone. Then she asked me what I thought had happened. It was almost as if she wanted me to take credit for it and flash a badge at her. That would mean her old man would have to give up the business and that she could give up being the double agent. It was just an impression, you understand, but what good is an undercover guy who can't trust his impressions?"

"So the little girl wants to get caught?"

"Big time. She also wants somebody stronger than she is to control her father. It's pretty classic."

I shrugged. He was pacing me perfectly.

"You're the counselor. You think you could turn her?"

He looked up and my motives were now transparent, but he was already half talked into it.

"You sonuvabitch. You set me up."

"You betcha. On the other hand, you're the one who keeps worrying about one of these clowns walking. We probably can't get the judge in this situation, so he gets disabled. We might be able to get McCain, but it's risky, so he gets disabled. But we have to leave a couple of the bad guys in good enough shape to lead Doug and Ron Gable to the K.C. players. The only problem is that we don't have much of anything on Lavelle, and I trust that Casey has covered his tracks better than anybody. He also has the bread to hire quality counsel. Enter Vivian."

"Lemme understand this. You want me to turn her before tomorrow night? You're going to give me a whole twenty-four hours? Thanks a lot, bud."

Cochise was agitated, but something about the proposition appealed to him because he was fighting with me and he could just as well have blown it off. I added fuel to the fire.

"All I want you to do is deliver Vivian to the lady cop just before the country club gig. I think Vivian's halfway there now. When I talked with Ketchum on Friday, he'd gotten an anonymous tip alleging that Casey was in up to his elbows. It was a female voice talking through a towel. Doug was pretty sure it wasn't Mimi. Sounds like something a kid in her kind of trouble would do. But then I'm not the psychologist."

I let it sink in. I wanted it to be irresistible to Galahad. It was.

"Okay. You set it up with Doug and I'll get her there. Now let's go get that package."

35

The Lexington airport is a typical rural airport with a few hangars and a gas pump. Thirty-three hundred feet paved with a grass crosswind strip. It was barely big enough to take a small corporate jet even if the pilot was real good at short-field procedures. At an altitude of 690 feet above MSL, it was in the low, flat river-bottom land just north of Lexington and the river and just off of Highway 13. It was used by sport jumpers, but there were no commercial operations there, so it functioned with a sporadically attended unicom, standard frequency. It is a no-frills port. But then, I was on a no-frills errand.

The Lear had hit and cleared Houston on schedule, according to Sergio, who left a message at the hotel. I left

Highway 13 to turn back east onto the county road, CC. The access road was paved for about a mile. As I turned onto the unpaved part and headed north, the back end broke loose and almost put us into the soybeans. A minute later we were ignoring the signs that said NO VEHICLES BEYOND THIS POINT, cruising past the hangars and the maintenance barn, and pulling the car up alongside the runway about dead center. I shut it down, blacked it out, found WHB on the radio again, and leaned the seat back. The air was pleasant and the crickets reminded me of nights spent crawdading with my cousins.

Little Brother was out of the car doing reconnaissance more out of habit than necessity. I looked out the window and tried to find Orion. Cochise was checking out the facilities—not a big job since they were limited to a large white frame maintenance barn and office building, an open pole barn strip hangar, a small house trailer, also white, and two secured T hangars belonging to Ferguson Aviation. I saw his shadowy figure checking out an old chopper without a rotor, a Beach B-18 without props, a Cessna twin with one wing propped up on a barrel and an artistically curved prop, indicating that it might have landed with the left wheel still tucked neatly up inside the wing.

We heard the high whine of the small jet before we saw it. It had just entered a regulation long downwind leg on approach. Two turns later the pilot was on a short full-flaps final. He snapped on the landing lights. Seconds later he set it neatly on the exact end of the runway and we could hear the thrust reversers being cranked. He swung it around deftly and turned onto the taxiway, pulling to a stop a few feet from the right front fender. It was a Gates Learjet Longhorn 29 with the distinctive wingtip vertical stabilizers. The engines continued to whine softly. Cochise appeared. The stairs were deployed and the courier/pilot emerged.

He walked over to us and, smiling, asked me for ID and the identity of my companion. He thought better of it, chuckled, and canceled the formal request with a sweep of his hand. Lawless had probably included that in his instructions. He was just a kid. He looked more like a baggage handler than a private pilot. But he was courteous and efficient. And he had really nailed the landing.

"Mr. Hopper."

I looked at the blond kid with my bullshit secret-agent look.

"Yeah?" I parried.

He grinned. "Mike told me to expect the worst. But I recognize your face from the pictures. I'm here with a diplomatic pouch, sir. I'll leave it with you and be on my way, unless there's anything else I can do."

"Yes, as a matter of fact, you can stop calling me sir. I'll take the pouch. And thank Mike when you get back to D.C."

"Yes, sir."

"And, by the way, that was a Top Gun landing."

"Thank you, sir. The Garretts we retrofit help on the short takeoffs. We replaced four of the seats with fuel tanks and they make the roll out a little longer. Doubles the range, though."

This was no ordinary corporate jet.

The kid reminded me of myself about the time I met Stryker Stephens. I thought about telling him that hooking up with the Lawlesses of the world was going to bring him grief, but you couldn't have convinced me of that at his age and I probably wouldn't have succeeded with him either. I felt real old. I saw Little Brother watching the whole scene from the shadows to which he had retreated. The boy pilot clambered back up the plane's stairs, the door whispered shut, then a minute or two later the Lear pivoted smartly and cruised to the end of the runway. Balls to the wall and with a mild roar, it disappeared into the night sky. Cochise sauntered over. I wanted to move. The unusual jet operation on this podunk strip might have drawn the kind of attention that we didn't need right now.

"Let's get out of here," I said. "We have a few details to arrange."

We drove back to the inn and checked the contents of the pouch. Cochise gave them the *Anarchist's Cookbook* seal of approval and asked me if he could meet Dave someday.

We began to do the stage blocking for the next day's event. Midway he called Casey's number. Casey answered the phone and Cochise hung up. He called again an hour later. I eavesdropped since I had a vested interest in the success of his adolescent seduction. This time he got the little lady of the manor and went into his most charming self.

"Vivian. It's Larry. Look, I know your old man's probably around, so I don't want you to say much. But I need to see you tomorrow. Something's come up and you're the only one who can help me with it, y'know. It's something important. Can you meet me at the Hideaway at about five o'clock?"

He paused and said nothing but "Uh-huh" for the next few moments.

"Well, I don't expect you to promise, babe. I just want you to do your very best to get there. If there were any other way to do this, I'd do it, but you're special and I know you can handle it. So I'm going to be looking for you, okay? Don't let me down, kiddo."

He hung up the phone and looked sick around the eyes.

"Well, is she going to be there?"

"I think so. I just paraphrased the stuff her old man's been saying to her in one way or another for most of her life. I think she'll be there. God, I hate it."

We refined the final points of the plan. It called for us

both to be clear of the country club by eight-thirty on Sunday evening. After that, whatever force looks after babies, drunks, malcontents, and mercenaries would hopefully give us a hand. I called Ketchum's place. I briefed him with the substantially fictitious plan and told him that we were going to try to deliver Vivian Casey to Tackleberry for a woman-to-woman chat about her father while the cocktail party was going on.

"I think she's your anonymous tipster, Doug, although it's just an intuition."

"If she is, we're a lot further along than I thought. Tackleberry is good at this stuff."

"Have dispatch ready to move on this in case the buy comes down. Or, for that matter, in case it doesn't."

"Better than that, good buddy. I'll be there. Shelley invited me. I gave her a little encouragement and she fell all over herself apologizing for overlooking law-enforcement representation at this community event. I'm backing you up, Hopper."

That changed the plan a little, but I thanked him for the thought and hung up.

"Okay, Little Brother. The Richmond PD in the person of one Chief Ketchum is going to be on-site. Adjust the details please."

"No problem. I may need you to decoy at some strategic moment, but as long as you keep your eyes on me, we shouldn't have any problem."

"Get some sleep."

"Hah! What kind of wuss do you take me for?"

"Stay off the whites, my friend. I need you naturally wired, not chemically altered."

"Please. You insult me."

He took the contents of the pouch for safekeeping and I went off into the dreamless sleep that occurs before curtain time for these dramas.

36

Sunday dawned warmer than expected for the season. I was missing Coal Creek and ready to go home. Or to Cabo, which is almost home.

By three in the afternoon I'd been all the way through two local papers, the Sunday *Kansas City Star*, *USA Today*, the *Wall Street Journal*, the Excelsior rag, and the *Richmond Times*. My eyes were saved by the fact that the newsstand was limited—no *Christian Science Monitor*. I had that sudden longing for control. Control is a useful story we tell ourselves to get over the sheer terror of how contingent our lives really are. I wanted to go see what Gaiters was doing in his big house with his family. I wanted to see whether Casey was hitting the whiskey bottle early. I wanted to know if Lavelle was making love to his wife and if the Mayor was dandling his grandson on his knee.

I didn't get into the T-bird to go look. Instead I did a series of mental gymnastics that serve as a substitute for sit-ups in terms of draining excess energy.

I was going to be on the ne'er-do-well side of formal for the Chamber of Commerce event, but in Richmond the outfit would do. Technically speaking, I hadn't been invited. I couldn't crash the party with Cochise because my cover was blown on the side of law enforcement, but his cover had to stay meticulously intact. He had to be one of "them." I wasn't going to walk in with Ketchum either. I was going to crash it solo and find Shelley Stone. Jim Farber was going to be on his way out of town and wanting to say good-bye to her, and having read about the event in the paper . . . blah, blah, blah. I had a small bet with myself that I could charm her.

My plane reservation back to Denver was made for Monday afternoon. If the operation went as planned, I needed to be *desaparecido* before Ketchum and the DEA launched the mop-up. Little Brother was out of there directly after the event for obvious reasons. No one would question his absence, or mine for that matter, except for the guilty, who would be in various stages of disarray.

The Denver Country Club is an elegant slate-gray, white-pillared old building. The Richmond country club is called the Shirkey Golf Club and looks more like a sprawling country contemporary with its slope-to-the-ground shake-shingle front and picture windows looking out at the golf course. It doesn't qualify as elegant, but it sets a certain tone.

I purposefully arrived forty-five minutes after Cochise said cocktails were to begin. No one stopped me at the cave-like door that formed a tunnel through the shingles. Apparently, if you were the kind of person who knew the event was happening, you were presumed to be an invitee. Like a homing pigeon, I flew straight to the side of Shelley Stone, who was playing grande dame of the evening in a black cocktail dress that could have made it in Denver, easy. White pearls, devoted husband at her side. He looked somewhat awkward, but he seemed to have a fine sense that this was her event, and I appreciated the way he looked at her. I went into action.

"Shelley."

She whirled around from her other conversation and looked at me quizzically. Then her face cleared.

"Why, Mr. Farber. Good to see you again. What does this mean? That you've decided to relocate your company here? If so, we're delighted."

"Well, Shelley, the eventual disposition of that plant is a problem I'm now going to hand over to my board of directors. I leave for Colorado in the morning and I just wanted to drop by to thank you for your help. And to have a drink, of course."

I do "boyish grins" pretty well and she got my very best. It didn't seem to matter that I wasn't going to be a feather in her cap this evening. She introduced me to her husband and pointed out Ketchum and McCain, who had taken up stations in other parts of the room. I thanked her and stopped at the hors d'oeuvre table before I got into serious mingling.

As cocktail hours went, this one bore a marked resemblance to most others of its ilk. The same people saying the same doodah to one another. The noise in the room was a low buzz. The ambitious looked over the shoulders of the people they were speaking with to see who else was there that they might better themselves by talking to. Cochise was deep in conversation with a young woman with a righteous cleavage, and I figured there wasn't any reason he shouldn't enjoy himself before the main event.

I walked over and stuck my hand in front of the Mayor, big as Dallas.

"Evening, Mayor McCain. I was just saying to Shelley Stone that I'm on my way back to Colorado and this seemed like as good a time as any to say thanks for your help. I don't know if we're going to be able to do any good here, but ..."

I let it trail off and McCain's eyes were boring holes through my head. Then it stopped and the jocular Mayor returned with full presence.

"Well, Jim, I do feel badly that we weren't able to be more persuasive. And, of course, we've had our share of trouble, what with poor old Luther and that fire at Casey's place. Sometimes I think my mayoral days ought to be over. This job seems to be losing some of its charm."

I didn't know whether he thought I had something to do with Luther Brock's death because I'd been observed by Brock's lackey at a crime scene or whether he was just relieved that the stranger was leaving so they could get on with their business.

I had one more touch to make and that was Gaiters, who I had never laid eyes on. I was debating whether to have Doug make an introduction when a better idea presented itself in the person of Roscoe E. Morton III. I walked over to the little table where he was sitting by himself somewhat forlornly, clapped his shoulder, and invited myself to join him.

"How's it going, Roscoe?"

Roscoe jerked around, startled. I hadn't talked to him since the debacle at Casey's and I had no idea what he'd been hearing around town.

"I'm doing fine, Jim. I really thought you'd left. Why haven't I heard from you?"

"Well, it's a little complicated, Roscoe. I'm going back to Colorado and let this all just ripen for a while. I'm not

entirely comfortable with what's going on in this town at
the moment. I think I'd like to see how it all turns out."

"Yeah, I understand, what with Luther and that motorcycle lady dyin' an' all. Still, seems like any town is sure
to have some of that, though. Guess it was just our turn."

Ever the booster, old Roscoe.

"Y'know, Roscoe, one of the people I didn't get to meet
was Judge Gaiters. I don't know if I'll be back to retrade
Casey on his land, but if Gaiters is the silent partner, it
might be worth making the contact."

Roscoe nodded his head agreeably. "Sure thing, Jim.
He's over there in the corner with his missus. Come on
along. I'll make the introduction."

When I saw the table we were headed for, I had about
ten seconds to take in Judge Gaiters in the privacy of my
anonymity. His hair was almost white, although he
couldn't have been more than fifty-five. I remembered
Mimi's description. The bony-kneed old fart with bad
breath. I wasn't close enough to detect the latter, but the
thought of his hands on her body drove the gall up into
my throat so that I had to start a deep-breathing exercise
halfway across the room in order to be able to speak civilly
when I got there. His wife was sitting demurely next to
him. She was a sweet-looking lady whose dark-haired good
looks had aged well. She had the look of a woman who
knew almost exactly what he was like and didn't want to
know the details because she believed there was nothing
she could do about it.

Roscoe went into his song and dance and Gaiters ap-
praised me with beady black eyes. Despite the social man-
tle that was his by virtue of position, there was something
deeply crass about him. I hated him on sight, but then
how could I not? We spoke pleasantries. His voice was
annoyingly whiny. It was over in an eye blink. I finished
up with Roscoe and went looking for Doug.

I found him at the bar and signaled for him to meet me out on the porch. We stepped out at different times and surveyed the golf course. The privacy was probably going to be short-lived.

"We finally got a break, Hopper."

"I'll take anything I can get, Doug. What's up?"

"When I left, Tackleberry and Vivian were sitting in my office. I didn't want to intrude, but my daughter's about that age, and when they cry like that, they're usually confessing something."

"I'm glad to hear it. We need more on Casey. But it doesn't change this game at all."

"I know. How's he going to time it?"

"The man's an artist. He'll start as soon as he spots an opportunity. Dinner starts at eight. I expect he'll make a first pass before then."

"Where are you going to be?"

"In first backup position. You're in second. We'd better get back in there."

I cased the room and I almost missed the key scene. I watched Cochise wandering into an unused banquet room with McCain. He closed the door behind them. I took up a post by the bar and just watched. They were in there for about ten minutes. During that time Jack Casey arrived with a flourish, and if he noticed me in the shadows, he didn't let on. I amused myself watching him work the room.

The banquet room door opened and only McCain came out. He walked over to Gaiters with that "Could I have a word with you?" demeanor. They got fresh drinks from a circulating cocktail waitress and then both went back into the banquet room.

My chest got tight and I was lost in a fantasy of what was going on in that room. I imagined Cochise pulling out his samples. Quietly. Carefully. In my mind's eye, I watched McCain pop the first one and Gaiters greedily going for the rest. It would be the standard public-relations drug gift offered, McCain and Gaiters would assume, by an ambitious city kid who'd heard about the Richmond connection in K.C. Or maybe he'd use St. Louis and stroke their ego with how famous they were becoming on the circuit.

And then it would be done. Was probably done as I was thinking the thought. Cochise had offered them a new and improved designer drug called the new Ecstasy and they were sampling it in the interest of business development and getting high. But although it looked and acted like Ecstasy, it wasn't. It was an aberration called MPTP, a slight chemical variation of MPPP that we named the Saint Louie Blues in honor of our good/bad guy from the city with the Arch and the Clydesdales. It had been prepared carefully in concentrations to do the job with a comfortable margin, far more potent than the street variety. Soon their brains would start to disintegrate. I would be back in Colorado before they got to the drooling stage.

I ordered another Jack and started to get impatient. I heard laughter from the banquet room. I was sorely tempted to grab Ketchum and just burst through the door and bag the two backwater bhagwans. I stifled it. The final result was to be much more satisfying.

The lady standing next to me was not hard to look at and I started some conversation about the mushroom festival. I caught Doug's eye and he was shifting from one foot to another, too. He was looking for some signal that it was time to move in and he wasn't going to get it. Not from me at least.

When the banquet room door opened, Little Brother strolled out and headed for the men's room. I followed. We had to wait for one of the guys to relieve himself of some Scotch before we could take our place at the urinals. Little Brother looked subdued.

"So?"

"No problem, bro."

"Anything else I need to know?"

"Yeah. I left Vivian Casey spilling her guts out at the police department."

"I heard. What about the hotshots?"

"It's done. I'm out of here. Has Ketchum figured it out yet?"

"I expect he has. I'll tell him that it just didn't get done."

"That's murder on my reputation. But I can live with that."

He packed his equipment back into his pants and looked at me.

"You okay, Cochise?"

"Yeah. I'm feeling pretty clean. They're even bigger assholes than I thought. Gaiters wanted to know if I could get him some young ass. Preferably colored. Jesus, Hopper, sometimes I think the sewer rats are winning. But thanks to you, it was open season on those bastards today."

"Thanks for your help."

He gave me five and he was gone. When I got back to the cocktail party, it looked normal but just barely. Ketchum was looking at me like I was Pontius Pilate. I went up to him because he was caught up with Shelley Stone, and it was safe to say that I was on my way and I'd be in touch. Very casual. Very brief. We could talk about the betrayal later. Maybe the friendship would survive and maybe it wouldn't.

It was another cold Missouri night and I put the T-bird in gear, ready to leave. Or flee.

37

Monday was a busy day. At eight A.M. Judge Leroy Gaiters was admitted to the Ray County Memorial Hospital for a complete evaluation of symptoms which included depression, difficulty breathing, and dizziness. By ten, Doug Ketchum had a warrant from the U.S. Attorney's Office for Jack Casey's arrest based on his daughter's allegations. She was in protective custody. By noon, the Mayor's secretary was canceling his appointments. He was having trouble walking. By two that afternoon, there was an investigative reporter down from Kansas City to cover the story that would almost break by the next morning.

At three P.M. the honorably discharged Lieutenant Brad Gikstra, also known as Geek, locked up his bar and headed on down the road on Arnie's old hard tail. At three-thirty, just before late checkout time, one of Ketchum's guys liberated the chemist from a motel room at the Rose Court on a tip from a long-distance caller who would not be identified and didn't talk long enough to be traced.

At exactly four-sixteen, Chief Douglas Ketchum of the Richmond PD made a phone call to Ron Gable at the EDA to thank him "for exactly nothing." At four forty-five, the District Attorney for Ray County put the barrel of his daddy's coon gun in his mouth and blew most of his brains out the back of his head. I didn't expect a resurrection this time either.

At five o'clock, I paid for an extra half-day and checked out of the Elms in Excelsior Springs, having avoided making any phone calls, including the one I owed Doug. I drove to Mimi's house. I intended to make it brief and catch an earlier plane.

When she answered the door, there was yet a third woman to know. Her face was almost healed. Her manner was calm and pensive. We didn't say anything at first. I put both arms around her and suppressed the impulse to croon something comforting. Arm in arm, we walked back into the same incongruous living room where the adventure had begun.

She shook her head at me as if to clear away the events of the past two weeks.

"So much has happened, Hopper."

"That's a fact. How are you?"

"I'm better, I think. Still in shock, I guess. I'm not sure what it all means."

I touched her again because I couldn't resist. If there was a way to make her deliberations easier, I wanted to find it, but my time was short. On purpose. We walked to the couch and sat. She put her head on my shoulder.

"I think it's over now, Mimi. I think you can leave this place. There's nothing to hold you. No heroes. No villains."

"Hopper, do you really know where Arnie is and you're just not telling me?"

"I know that I told him to leave and not look back. Where he is now and what he will do is anybody's guess. I don't think you can be responsible for him anymore."

She ran her hand across my chest. I stayed cool on the outside and felt my heart jump on the inside.

"I can't imagine it. I just can't imagine it. And I don't know where to go and what to do next."

I traced the arc of her eyebrow and she closed her eyes.

"Wherever it is, it has to be good for you. Take your time. Your life has been radically changed. Nobody expects you to figure it out in the first five minutes. If you need someplace to think ... "

She laughed softly into my shoulder. "I can always look you up, right?"

"Right. Come to Cabo or Denver and we'll spend some time. Time, Mimi. It's the only resource any of us really have. Don't waste any more of yours."

She murmured something that I couldn't hear. It looked like I was going to miss that early flight.

EPILOGUE

It was Lucia's night off, so Stryker was doing the honors.
The snapper was fresh off his own boat. Sergio was expected for dessert and Maggie's arrival was also predicted
"sometime." Maggie happened when Maggie happened.
Now it was time for me to report.

Stryker pronounced the sauce "acceptable." He flung a
basket of fresh tortillas on the table and looked at me
patiently. And then he stopped being patient.

"You've heard from Ketchum?"

I made sure I had heard from him. As soon as I'd landed
at Stapleton, I'd retired to the relative privacy of the Red
Carpet Club and once again abused my phone credit card.

I was silent. Still thinking of Mimi and Arnie and Parkinson's disease.

"Bullfrog, I am not going to beg for information. And
that is final. If you wish to discuss this incident, let us do
so with some efficiency. If you want to hoard your secrets,
I will have a Courvoisier and ignore you."

"I'm sorry, Professor. He tells me that Vivian Casey is a sterling witness. The feds are doing mop-up and the chemist is happy being State's witness. Doug thinks the cases will get to trial in about eighteen months."

"And the disabled?"

"Nobody has filed on them because they're . . . disabled. He never really asked about it."

Stryker grunted.

"And what of the operative?"

"He called three days later. Told me a few jokes. I gave him the latest. He had no comment. This whole thing is marked by silence, Stryker."

"And better left that way, perhaps."

"Has anyone corresponded with the Foundation?"

"I left that for Sergio to do with Mike Lawless. He tells me that the first informant is impressed with your success. He notes that Burroughs is satisfied that his money was well spent. But none of that matters a tinker's damn if I correctly read the look on your face. What's the matter, bullfrog? You have reservations about the outcome."

I left the table and settled myself down on a sturdy redwood chaise lounge on the deck. He joined me there a minute later, the threatened Courvoisier palmed in his broad hand.

"It was only one little rat's nest in a small Missouri town. How many of them are there? If we blow up one lab in Richmond, will two more pop up somewhere else? How long do we fight this war, Stryker? As long as Korea? As long as Nam? And with the same damned results?"

Stryker sighed, a sign that my questions had become onerous and unanswerable.

"Longer than any other war, I suspect. But a war is a war, Hopper. If you enter it in good faith, you fight it until it's over. There are always choices. Give it up, if it bothers you too much."

215

I declined the gambit. He drank his cognac.

"I do have one last question, Hopper."

"So ask."

"When Cochise took out the lab, there were two arsonists. One presumably was Cochise. And the other?"

"It was Doug. He was an ordnance specialist in Nam. Those guys could carve their initials on a tree or take out a city with C4. No one is going to talk about it. There's no need."

"Interesting."

It was over. The surf provided background music, but the music was bittersweet.